Science in Infographics

FORCES

Jon Richards
and Ed Simkins

Gareth Stevens
PUBLISHING

Please visit our website, www.garethstevens.com.
For a free color catalog of all our high-quality books,
call toll free 1-800-542-2595 or fax 1-877-542-2596.

Cataloging-in-Publication Data

Names: Richards, Jon. | Simkins, Ed.
Title: Forces / Jon Richards and Ed Simkins.
Description: New York : Gareth Stevens Publishing, 2020. | Series: Science in infographics | Includes glossary and index.
Identifiers: ISBN 9781538242995 (pbk.) | ISBN 9781538243022 (library bound) | ISBN 9781538243008 (6 pack)
Subjects: LCSH: Force and energy--Juvenile literature. | Information visualization--Juvenile literature.
Classification: LCC QC73.4 R47 2020 | DDC 531'.6--dc23

Published in 2020 by
Gareth Stevens Publishing
111 East 14th Street, Suite 349
New York, NY 10003

Printed in the United States of America

CPSIA compliance information: Batch #CS19GS: For further information contact Gareth Stevens, New York, New York at 1-800-542-2595.

CONTENTS

4–5 GRAVITY

6–7 USING GRAVITY

8–9 RUBBING TOGETHER

10–11 STREAMLINING AND RESISTANCE

12–13 GETTING FASTER

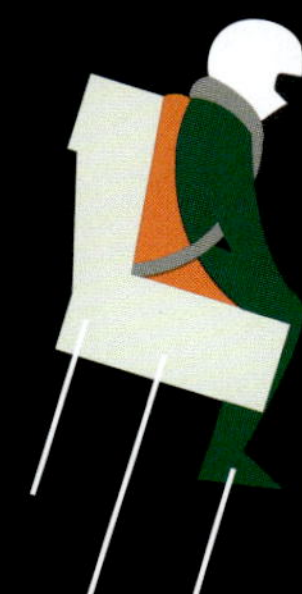

14–15 PRESSURE

16–17 USING PRESSURE

18–19 LEVERS AND WEDGES

20–21 RAMPS AND SCREWS

22–23 WHEELS AND PULLEYS

24–25 ATOMIC FORCES

26–27 MAGNETS AND MAGNETISM

28–29 USING MAGNETS

30–31 GLOSSARY & WEBSITES

32 INDEX

GRAVITY

When you throw something up into the air, you know that it will fall back down to Earth. This is caused by a force known as gravity and it affects everything in the universe.

MASS AND WEIGHT

Your mass is the amount of "stuff" you are made out of and it stays the same wherever you go. Your weight measures how much gravity is acting on you and it changes as the force of gravity changes.

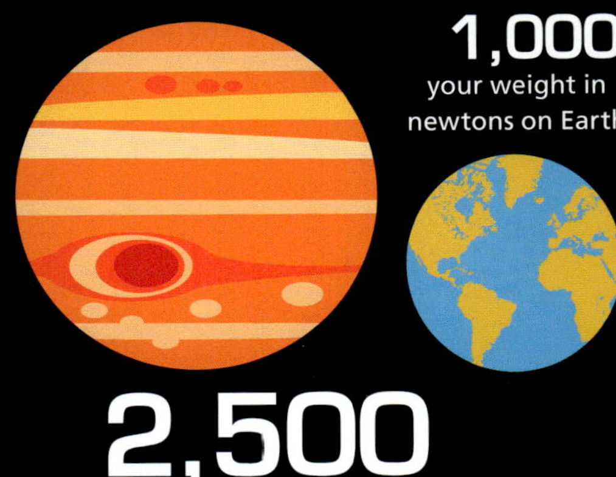

Weight is measured in units called newtons.

Mass uses units such as kilograms.

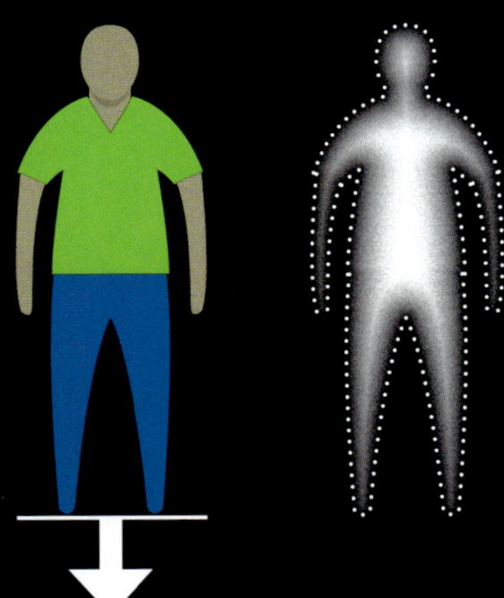

Any object that has mass has a gravitational force that will attract any other object with mass. This is why we stay on Earth's surface and don't fly off into space. Objects with more mass have a greater force of gravity. **The force of gravity on Jupiter is more than 2.5 times greater than that on Earth.**

INTO ORBIT

If an object is traveling fast enough it will start to go around Earth in a path called an orbit. The speed needed to orbit depends on the altitude of the object – the object has to move faster when it is closer to the surface of Earth.

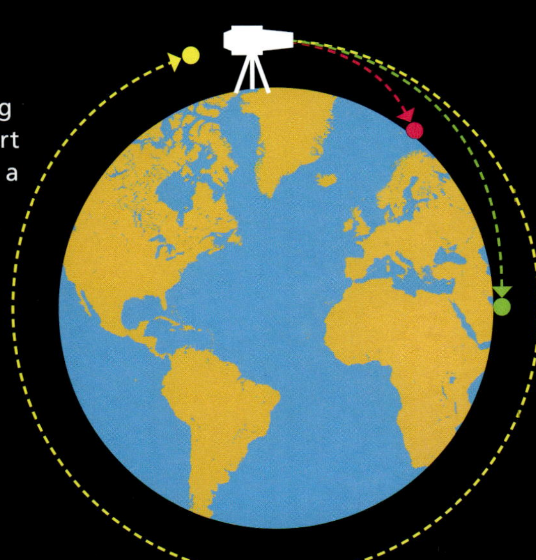

At an altitude of 22,236 miles (35,786 km), a satellite will orbit Earth once every 24 hours, so it will stay above the same point on the surface. **This is called a geostationary orbit.**

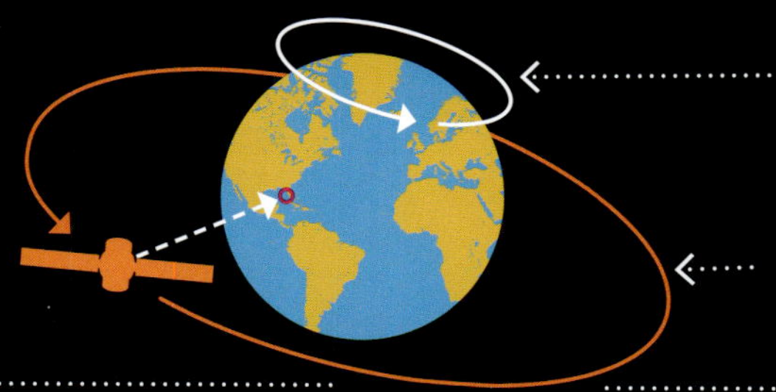

Planet orbits

As well as keeping satellites in orbit around Earth, gravity keeps the planets orbiting the sun. Those closer to the sun have to orbit much faster than those farther away.

ORBITAL VELOCITY (MILES/SECOND)

The planets do not orbit in circular paths. Instead, their orbit follows a stretched circle, called an ellipse.

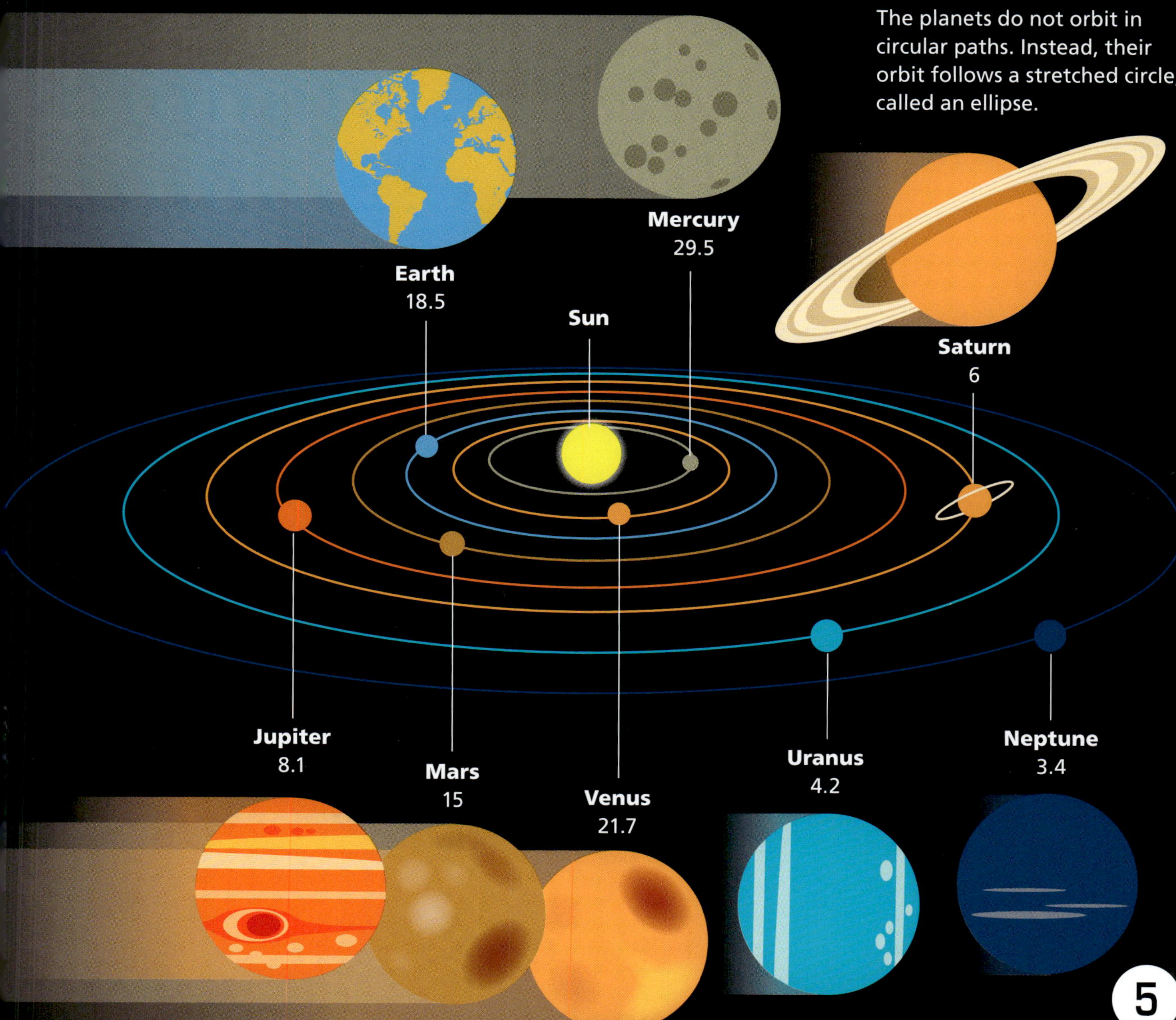

USING GRAVITY

While overcoming gravity makes it difficult for us to send objects out into space, we can use it to produce electricity, explore outer space, and discover distant worlds.

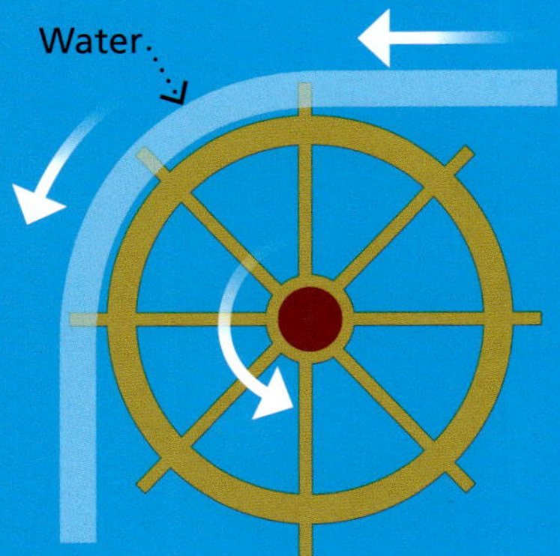

A water mill uses flowing water to turn a large wheel. In the past, water mills were used to grind corn and to power factories.

WATER POWER

Thanks to gravity, water always flows downhill. People have been using this fact for hundreds of years to help with work and to make electricity.

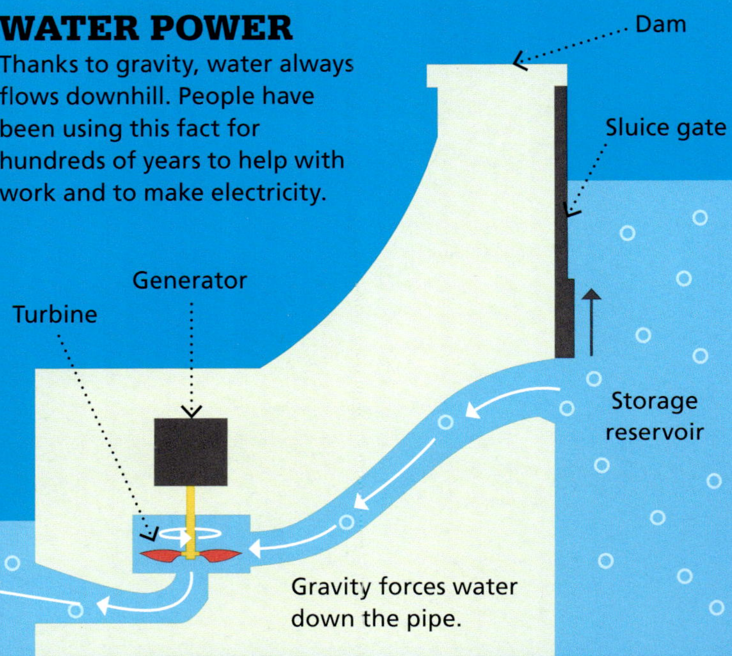

HYDROELECTRIC POWER STATION

Power stations use flowing water to produce electricity. Tidal power stations use the daily variation of the tides. Hydroelectric dams create large artificial lakes behind them. Gravity then pushes the water down through large pipes so that it flows past large, bladed wheels called turbines. The spinning turbines are connected to generators, which produce electricity (see above).

Overcoming gravity

To blast clear of Earth and reach space, you need to use a powerful rocket. These burn fuel with oxygen to produce a powerful blast of gas that pushes a rocket forward.

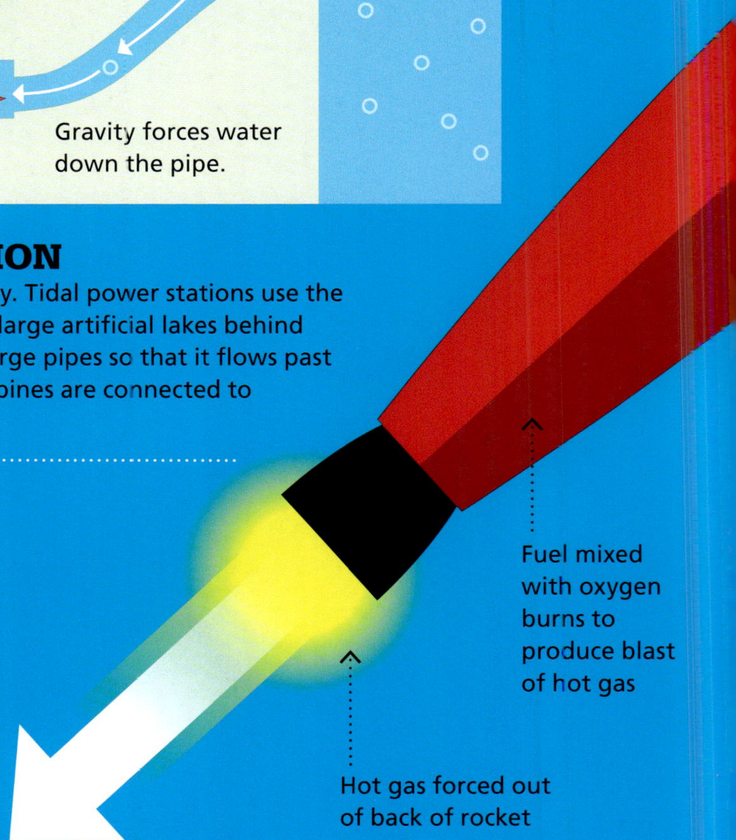

36,000

The speed in miles per hour that NASA's *New Horizons* spacecraft blasted off from Earth on its way to Pluto.

Slingshots

Traveling to distant planets in the solar system takes a lot of energy. But a spacecraft can get a helping hand by flying close to another planet. As it does so, the gravity of the planet speeds the spacecraft up, acting like a slingshot to fling it faster toward its destination.

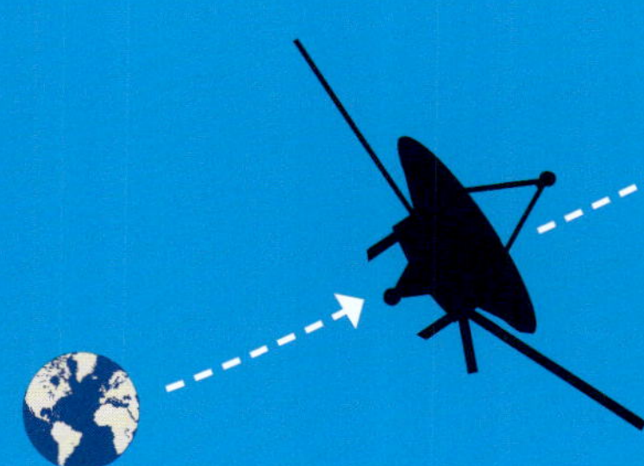

Distant planets

All objects with mass attract other objects, even if they are much smaller. As a result, as the planets orbit the sun, they pull the sun back and forth. Astronomers use this fact when trying to find planets orbiting other distant stars.

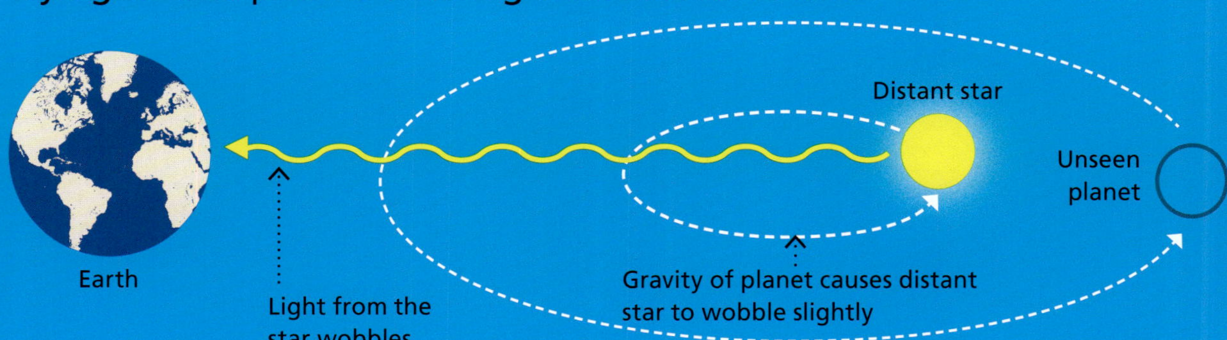

RUBBING TOGETHER

When two substances rub together, they produce a force called friction. This force can make it harder to move objects, but it is very helpful when slowing things down.

UP CLOSE

Friction is a force that occurs when two substances move, or try to move, against each other. It acts in the opposite direction to the movement.

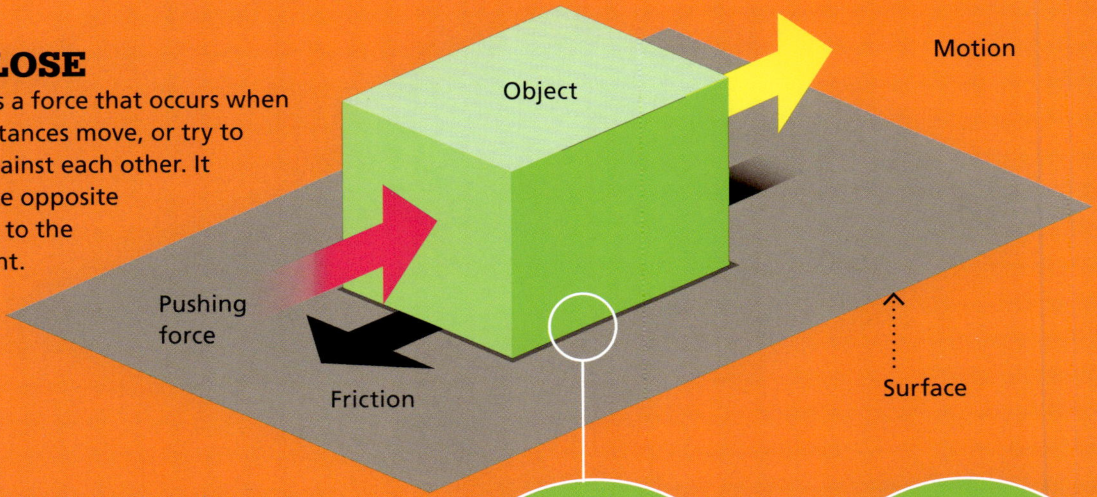

ROUGH AND SMOOTH

The amount of friction depends on how rough or smooth the two substances are. Rough substances will increase the amount of friction, while smooth substances will reduce the amount.

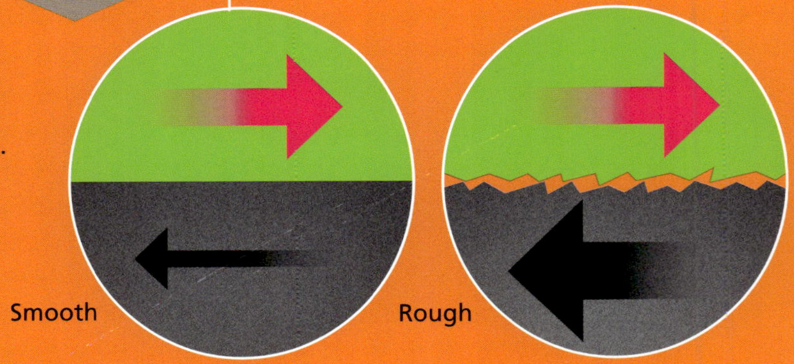

Lubrication

To make substances move more smoothly and reduce friction, lubricants, such as oil, are used. The lubricant lies between the two substances, allowing them to slide over each other more easily.

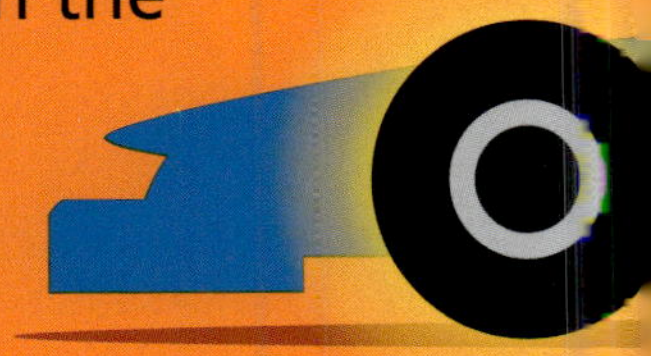

SKATING

The blades on ice skates are very thin, so they increase the pressure when you stand on them on ice. This higher pressure melts a little of the ice and creates a thin layer of water, which reduces friction, allowing a skater to glide easily over the ice.

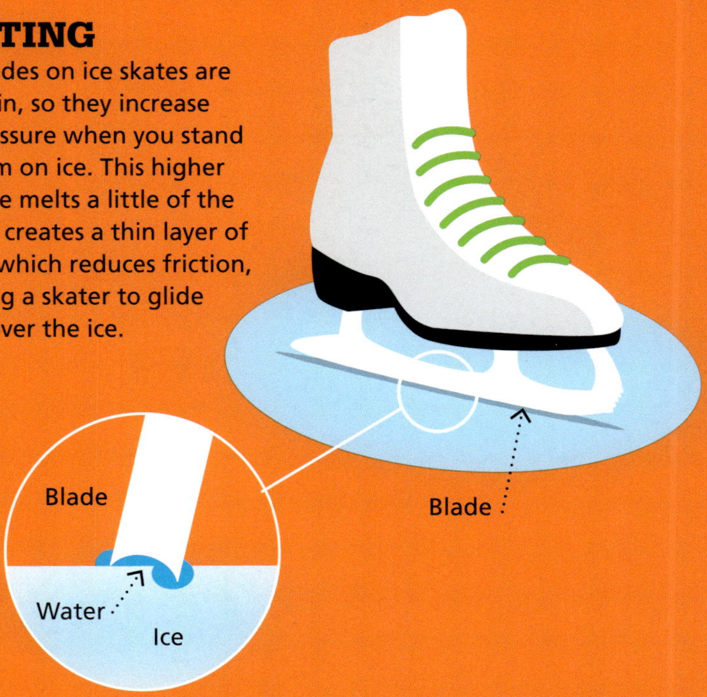

Wheels

Wheels reduce friction because they don't rub against the ground. Instead, they roll over its surface.

USING FRICTION

Car and bike brakes work by pushing pads against the spinning wheel, or a disc attached to the wheel. This increases friction, slowing the car or bike down.

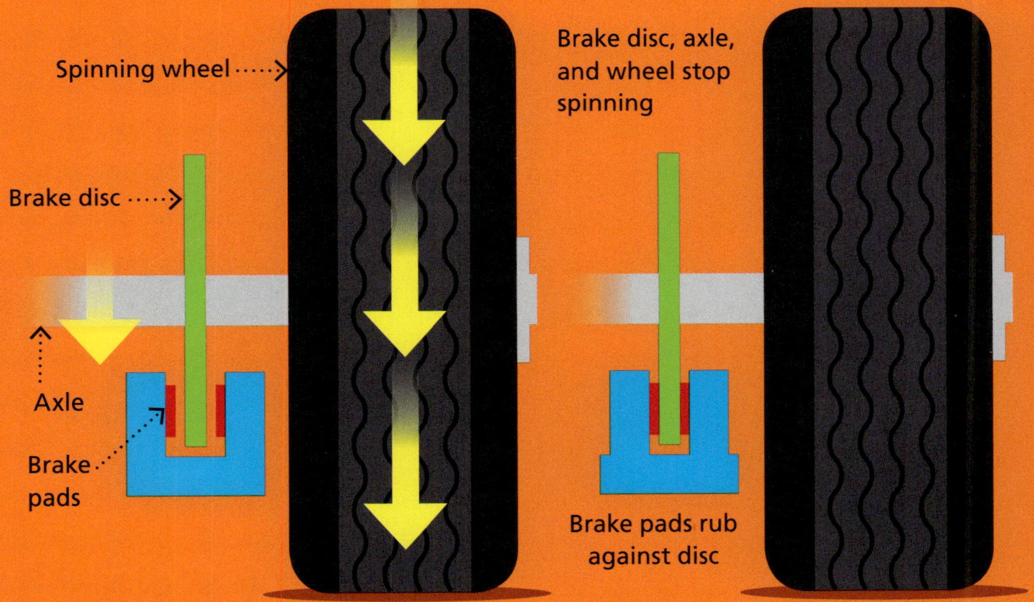

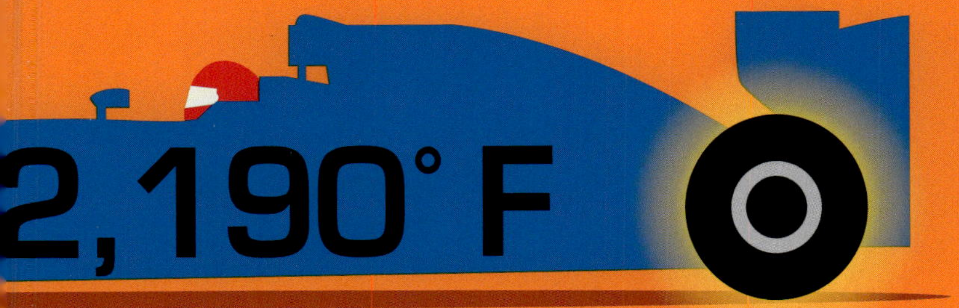

This is the temperature that the brakes on Formula One cars are designed to withstand. That's hot enough to melt gold!

STREAMLINING AND RESISTANCE

Moving through air and water can be difficult, especially if an object is the wrong shape. Changing its shape can make water and air pass over an object more easily, allowing it to move faster and more efficiently.

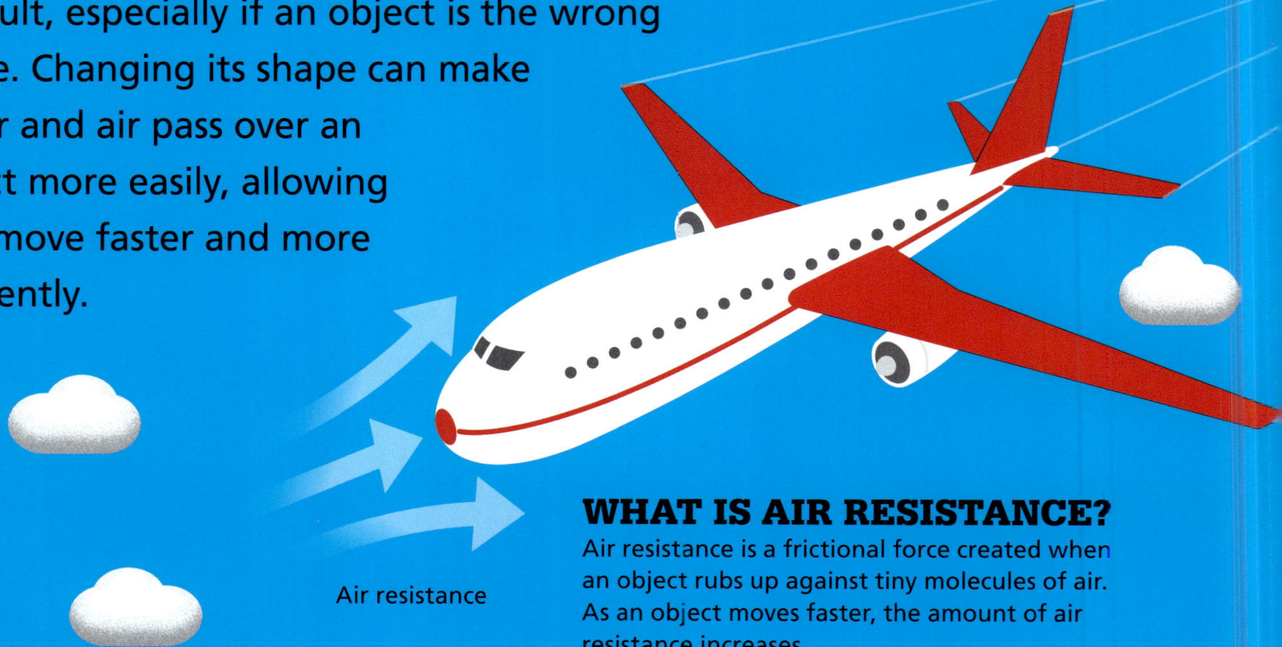

WHAT IS AIR RESISTANCE?

Air resistance is a frictional force created when an object rubs up against tiny molecules of air. As an object moves faster, the amount of air resistance increases.

Overcoming air resistance

To decrease air resistance, an object can have a special streamlined shape. A bullet or a fast car has a pointed nose, smooth curves along the body, and a specially shaped back so that air passes over it easily.

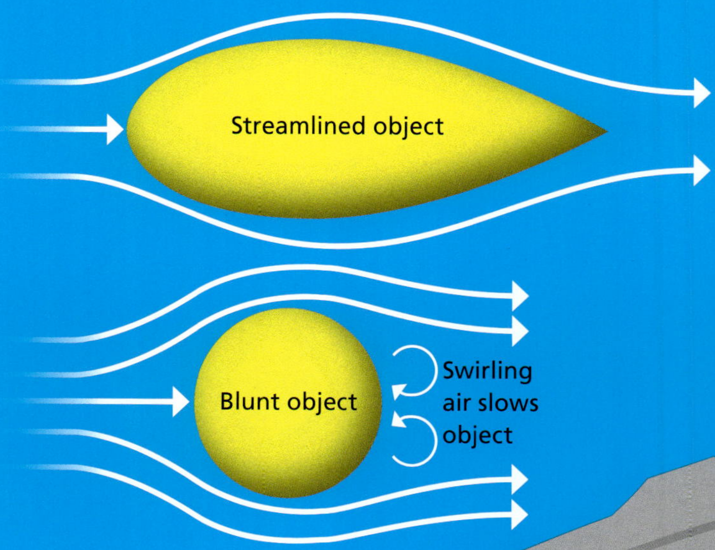

USING AIR RESISTANCE

Air resistance can be helpful when it comes to slowing things down. A skydiver has a parachute to increase the air resistance and slow their fall down to a safe speed, while a drag racer or some fighter jet pilots use parachutes to slow down their vehicles.

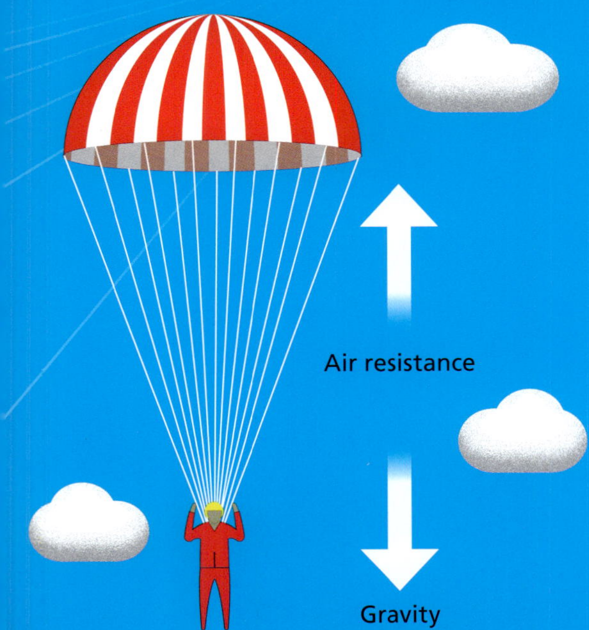

Water resistance

Moving through water is even harder than moving through air. Boats and ships have a number of ways of reducing this force so they can move faster and more easily.

A catamaran has two hulls that lift the body of the boat out of the water.

A trimaran has three hulls that lift the body of the boat out of the water.

A hydrofoil has an underwater wing that lifts the body of the boat out of the water.

Feather and weight

If you dropped a feather and a hammer at the same time, the feather would fall more slowly because air resistance slows its fall. However, if you dropped them in a vacuum (such as on the moon, as one astronaut did in 1971), they would fall at the same speed because there is no air resistance.

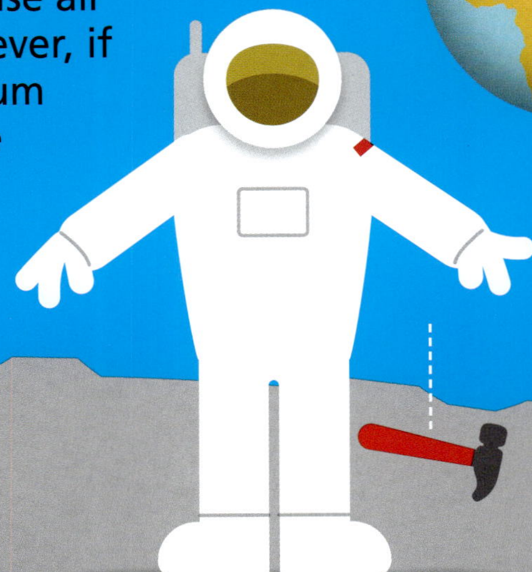

GETTING FASTER

If no force acts on an object, it will either stay still or move along at a constant speed. If you add a force, such as accelerating or braking, the object's speed may increase, it may change direction, or even both.

FASTER AND SLOWER

Gaining speed and becoming faster is known as acceleration, while becoming slower is known as deceleration (or by scientists as negative acceleration).

FALLING TO EARTH

Gravity causes objects to accelerate toward the surface of a planet. Differences in gravity cause objects to fall at different rates on different planets (see page 4).

32.15 FT/S^2

The rate of acceleration due to gravity on Earth.

ft/s^2 is feet per second per second – so after 1 second an object is falling at 32.15 feet per second, after 2 seconds it is falling at 64.3 feet per second, after 3 seconds it is falling at 96.45 feet per second, and so on.

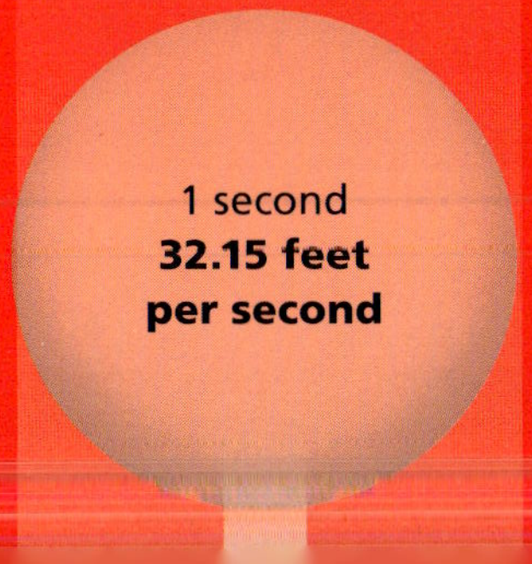

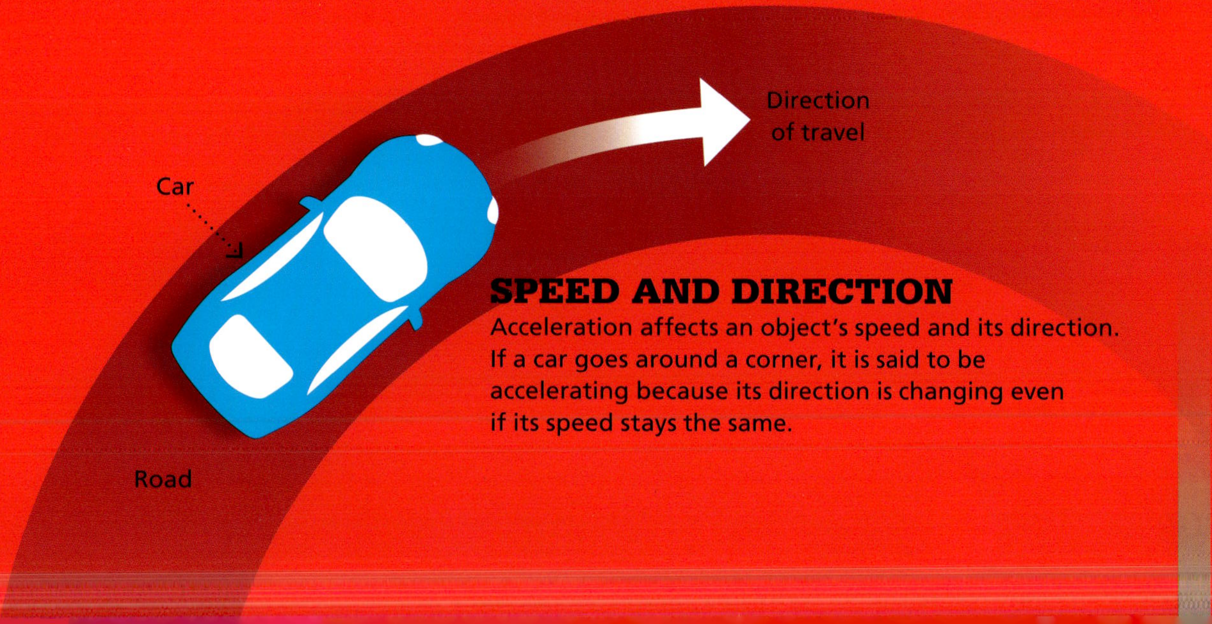

SPEED AND DIRECTION

Acceleration affects an object's speed and its direction. If a car goes around a corner, it is said to be accelerating because its direction is changing even if its speed stays the same.

ACCELERATION RATES (FT/S^2)

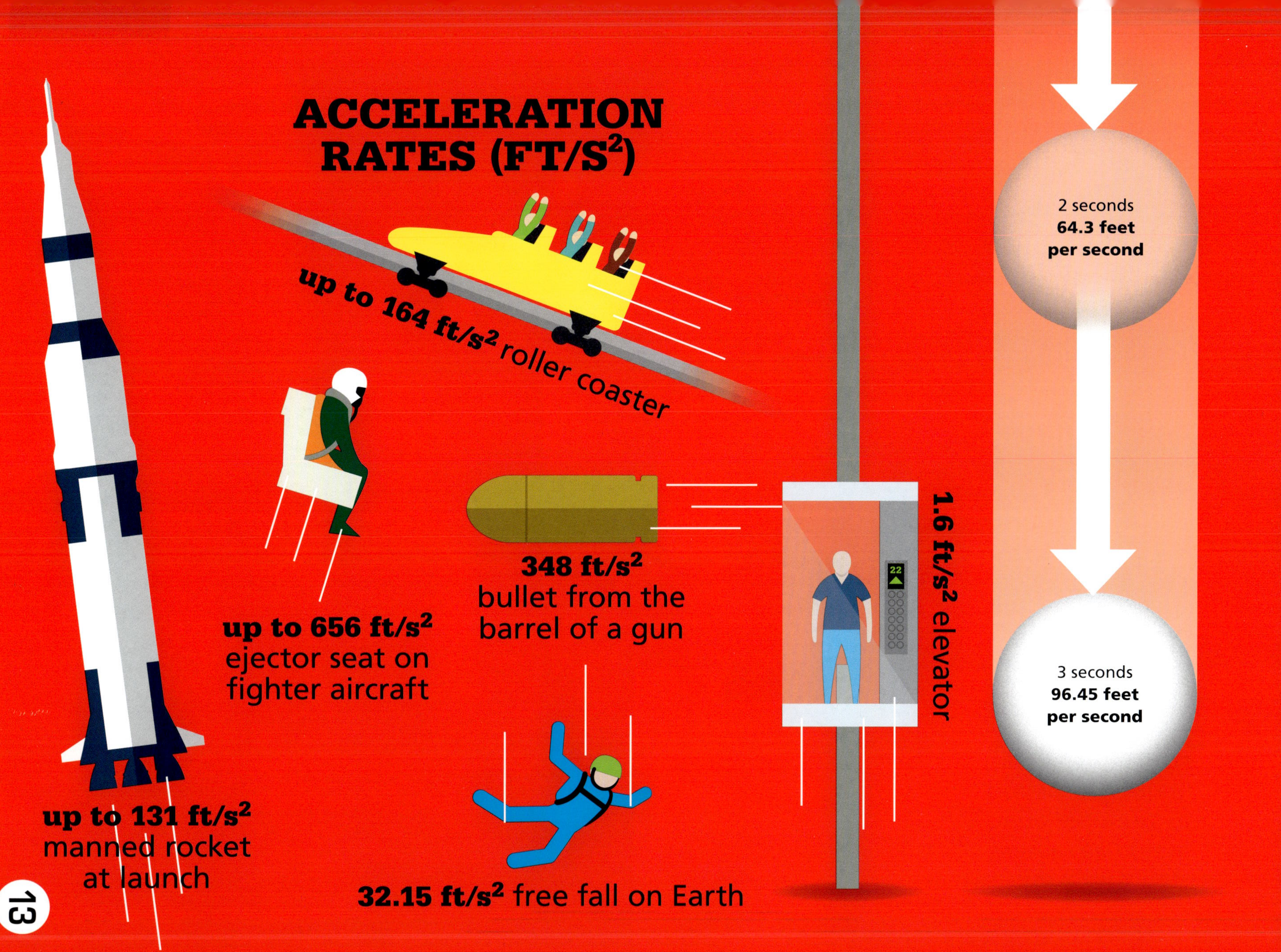

PRESSURE

Pressure is a force that is caused by objects pushing against each other. This can be the force of the atmosphere pushing down on you, the prick of a sharp needle, or the crushing forces deep in the ocean.

114,800 ft
Atmospheric pressure is one-hundreth of that found at sea level.

65,600 ft
Atmospheric pressure is less than one-tenth of that found at sea level.

33,000 ft
Atmospheric pressure is so low that aircraft flying at this height have pressurized cabins so people can breathe easily.

CHANGING PRESSURE

A force exerts pressure on any surface. The greater the force, the greater the pressure.

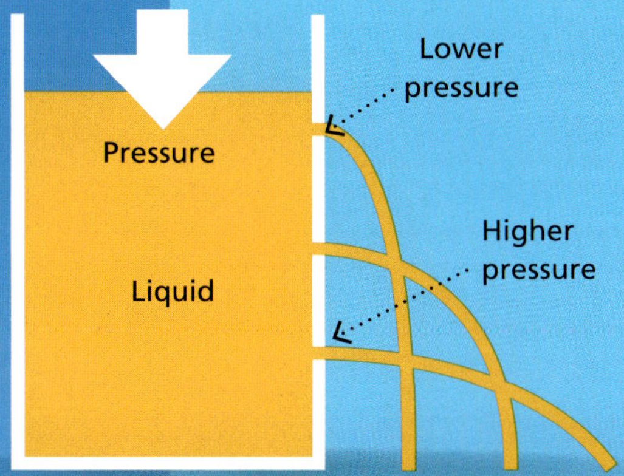

Pressure is also affected by area. If the force is acting over a large area, then the pressure will be low. If it is acting over a small area, then the pressure will be higher.

Pressure and depth
Water can create huge amounts of pressure down in the ocean depths.

0 ft (sea level)
Atmospheric pressure is normal.

33 ft
Pressure is double that found at sea level.

400 ft
Depths divers can reach without special suits.

29,000 ft
The air around the peak of the tallest mountain on Earth is so thin that climbers need to carry their own oxygen supply with them.

Pressure and altitude

Air has mass and it pushes down on you all the time, creating a force called atmospheric pressure. The higher up you go, however, the less air there is, so atmospheric pressure reduces with height, or altitude.

ONE TON
The approximate force of the air pushing down on you now.

0 ft (sea level)
Atmospheric pressure is normal, but varies as the weather changes (see pages 16-17).

21,000 ft
Submersibles need superstrong hulls to withstand high pressure.

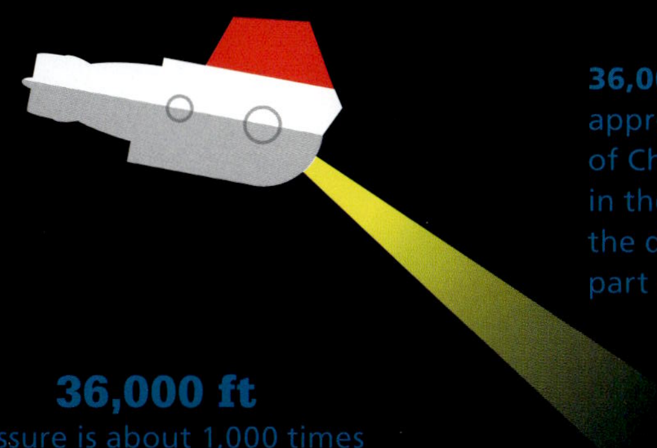

36,000 ft The approximate depth of Challenger Deep in the Pacific Ocean, the deepest known part of the oceans.

36,000 ft
Pressure is about 1,000 times greater than at sea level.

USING PRESSURE

We can use changes in pressure to move objects and material, to get off the ground, to see how our bodies are performing, and to predict what weather conditions are heading our way.

HYDRAULICS

Diggers and other machines squeeze liquids inside pipes to move hydraulic rams and operate digging arms of lifting booms.

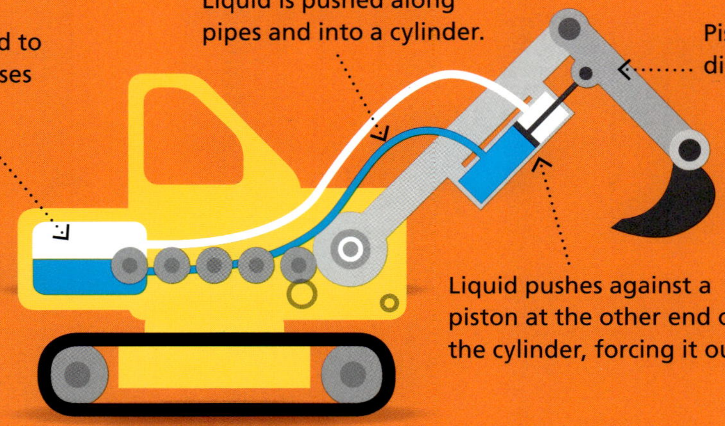

Air pressure and weather

As the air warms up and cools down, the force it pushes down on Earth changes. This force is known as air pressure and changes in it tell us what weather may be coming.

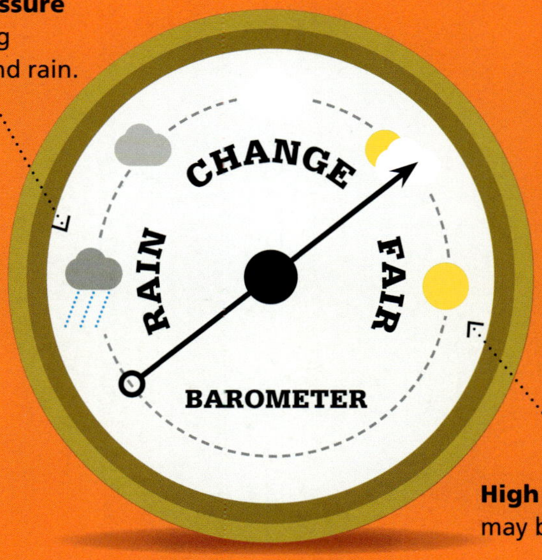

STAYING ON THE GROUND

Race cars are fitted with wings like those on aircraft, but positioned upside down. These wings produce a downwards force, called downforce, to push the race car into the track and to stop it from sliding as it zooms around corners.

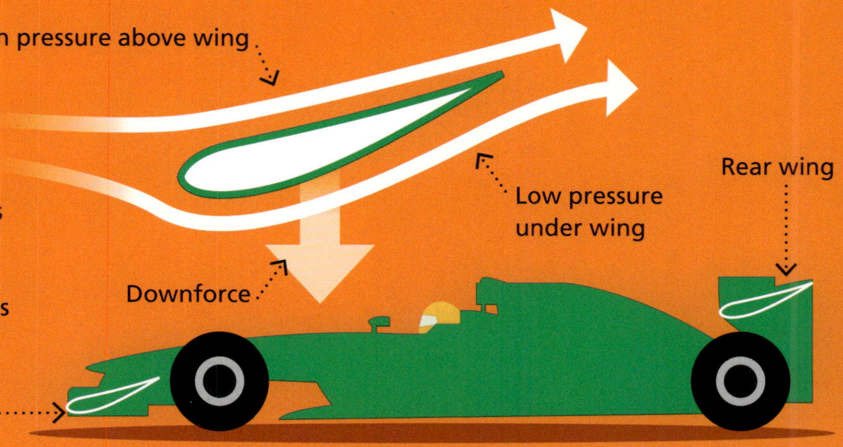

GETTING OFF THE GROUND

Aircraft use specially shaped wings to help get them off the ground, producing a force called lift.

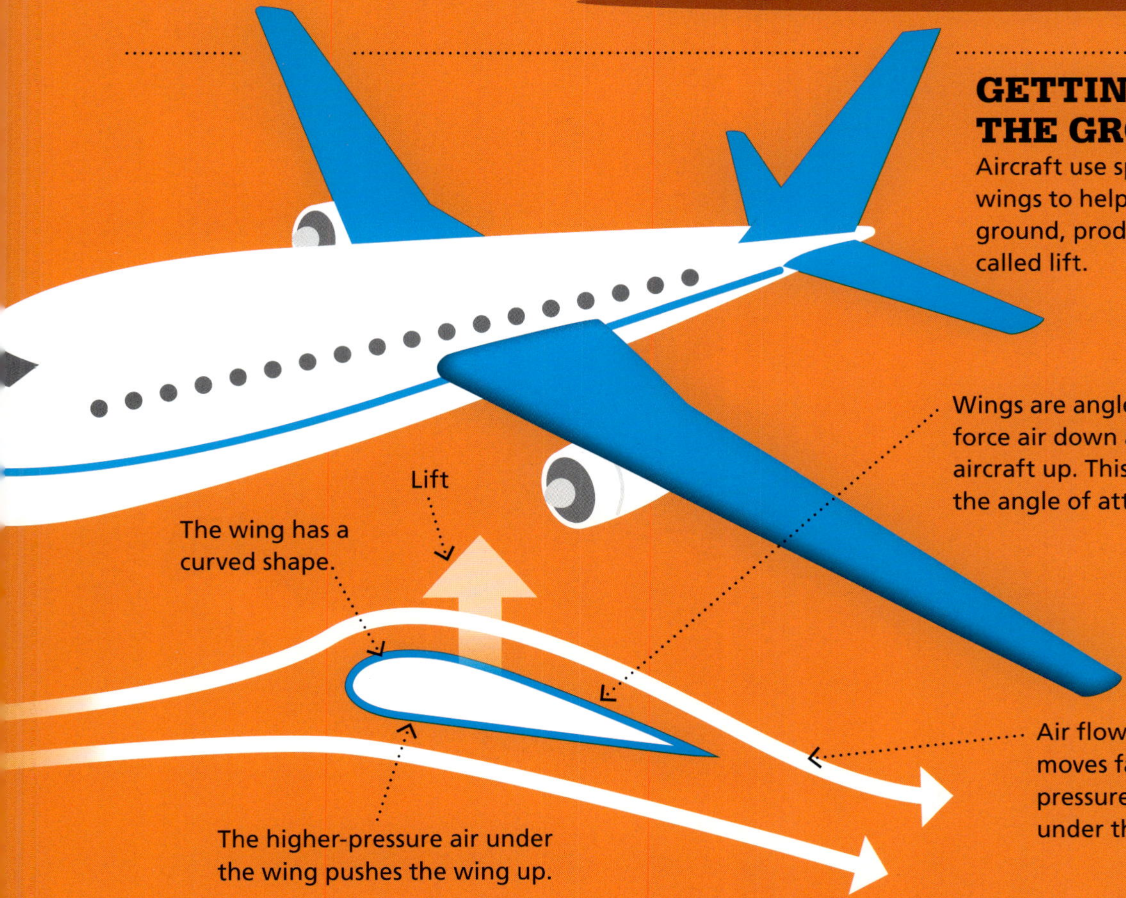

INCREASING PRESSURE

Sometimes it's helpful to increase pressure. A thumbtack has a large, flat head to push against. This pushing force is transmitted to a small point, increasing the pressure greatly so the pin can force its way into the surface.

DECREASING PRESSURE

At other times, it's helpful to reduce pressure. Tractors are fitted with large tires. Their weight acts over a larger area than normal tires, reducing the pressure so that they don't sink into mud or damage soil.

LEVERS AND WEDGES

Levers and wedges are simple machines that use forces to move objects, making it easier for us to lift things or push them along.

LEVERS

Levers use a beam or rod and a pivot, also called a fulcrum, around which a force acts, making the force of the effort greater. There are three types of lever. The type of lever depends on the arrangement of effort, fulcrum, and the load being moved.

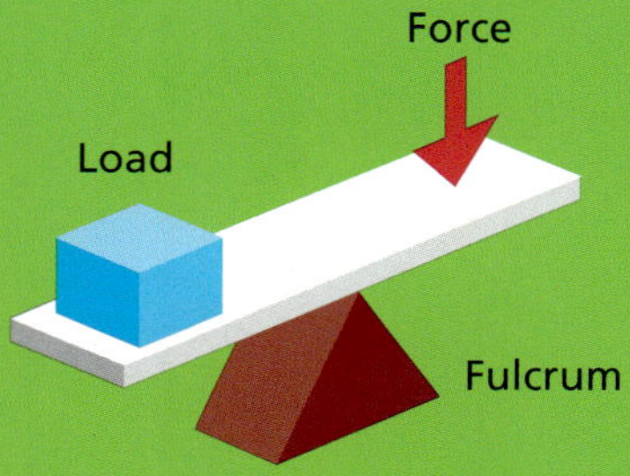

Class one lever

The fulcrum is put between the load and the effort. An example is a trolley.

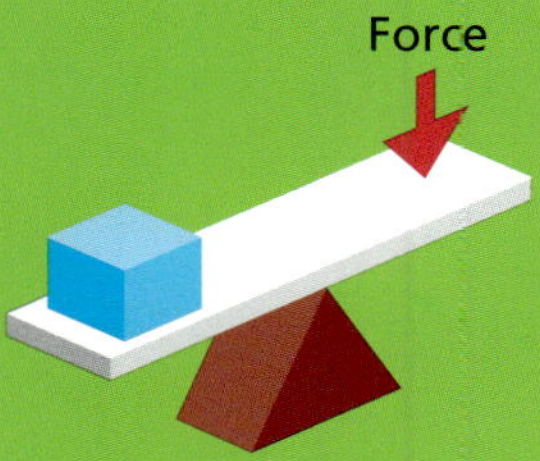

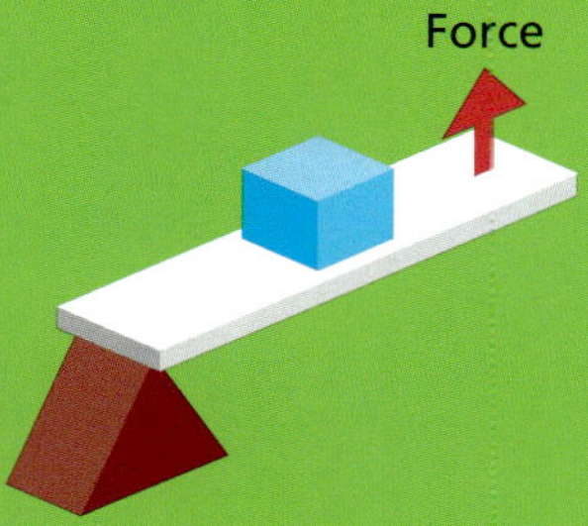

Class two lever

The fulcrum and effort are at either end, with the load in the middle. An example is a wheelbarrow.

Class three lever

The load and the fulcrum are at either end and the effort is in the middle. An example is a fishing rod pulling a fish out of the water.

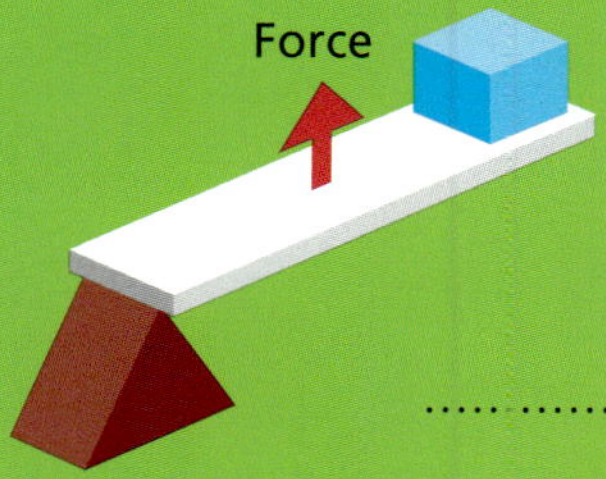

Turning forces and moments

The turning effect of a force around a fulcrum is called a moment. Levers change the effect of a moment by changing the distance between the effort and the fulcrum.

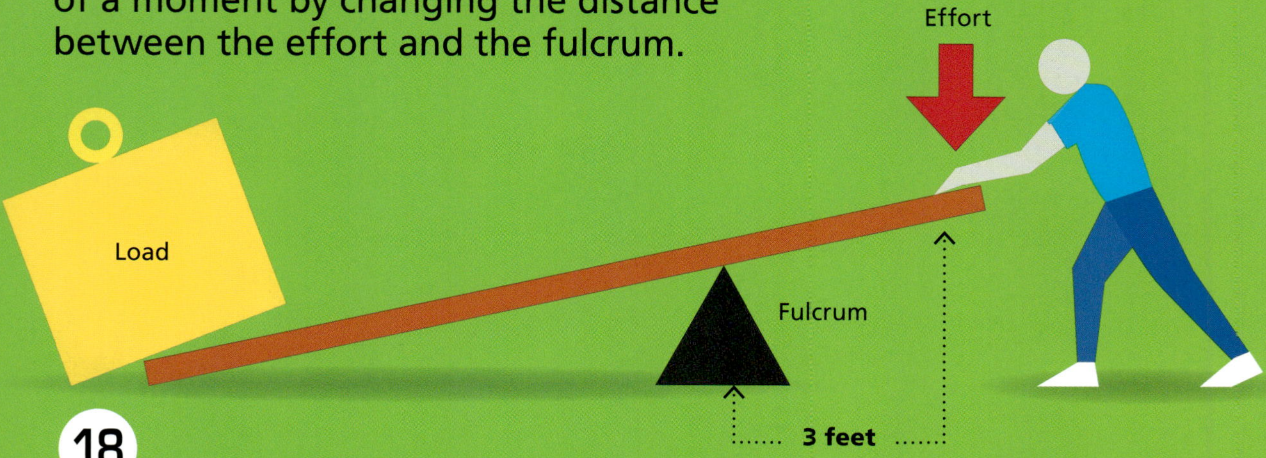

WEDGES

A wedge is a triangular machine with a pointed end and a blunt end. When a force is applied to the blunt end, the force is then transferred to the point as well as sideways.

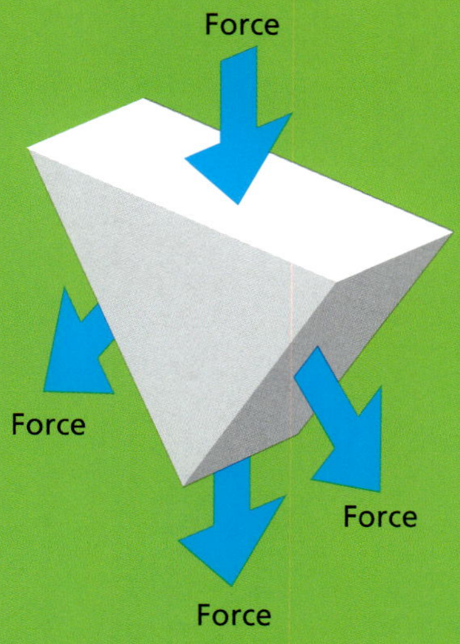

Wedges are used to ...

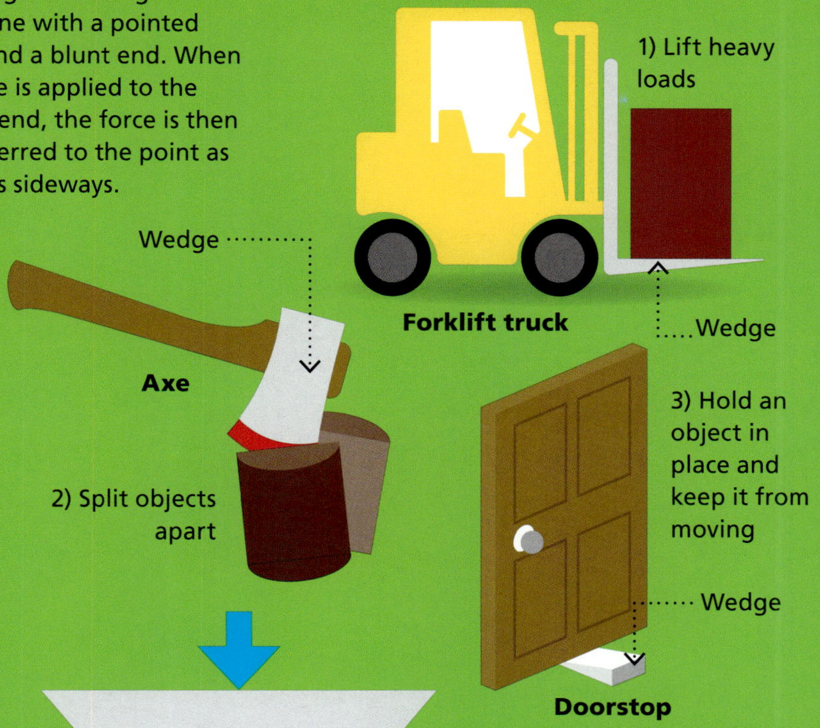

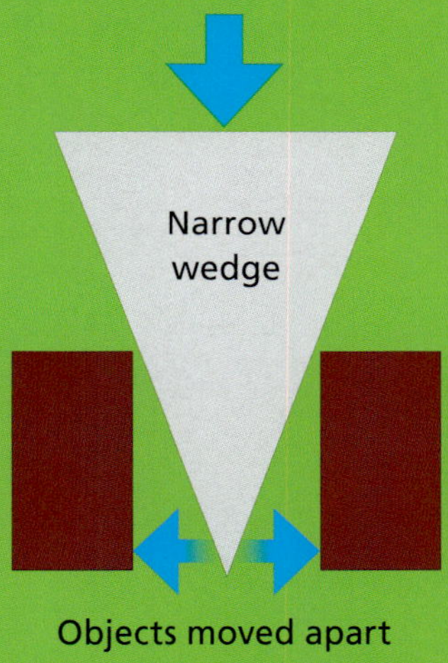

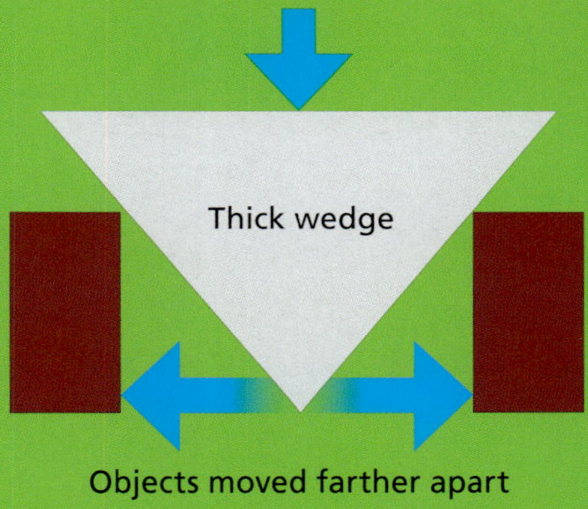

A narrow wedge is easier to drive in and push things apart than a thicker one, but you have to push the narrow wedge in farther to complete the task.

An effort acting over a short distance will have less effect than an effort acting over a large distance. This is why it is easier to undo a nut using a wrench than it is using your fingers, for example.

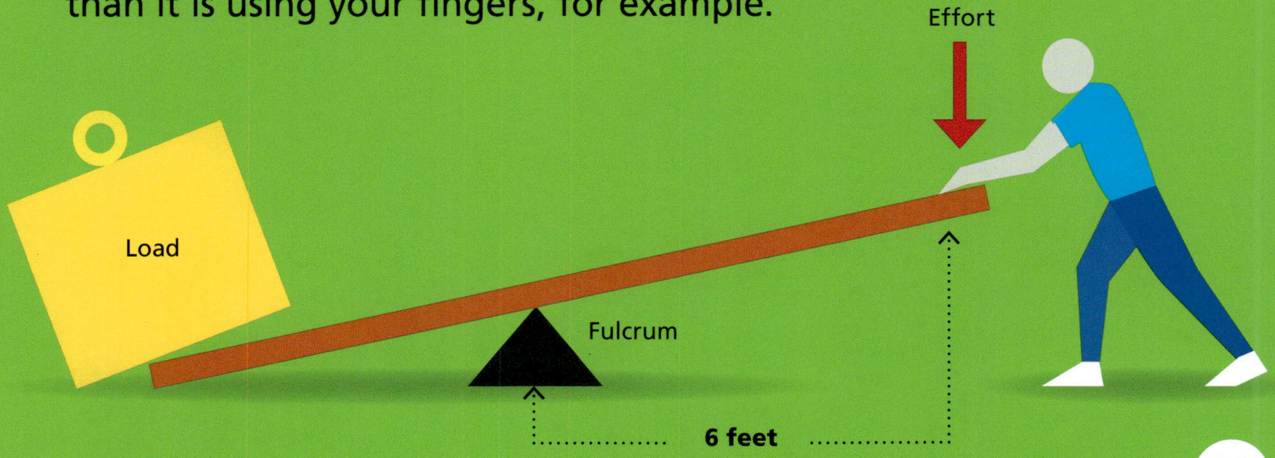

RAMPS AND SCREWS

Ramps are also known as inclined planes. They are used to make it easier to raise objects. Screws are simply inclined planes that are wrapped around a central core.

Inclined planes

An inclined plane is a triangle shape where one end is higher than the other. It takes less force to move an object up an inclined plane than by raising the object vertically, but the distance traveled is greater.

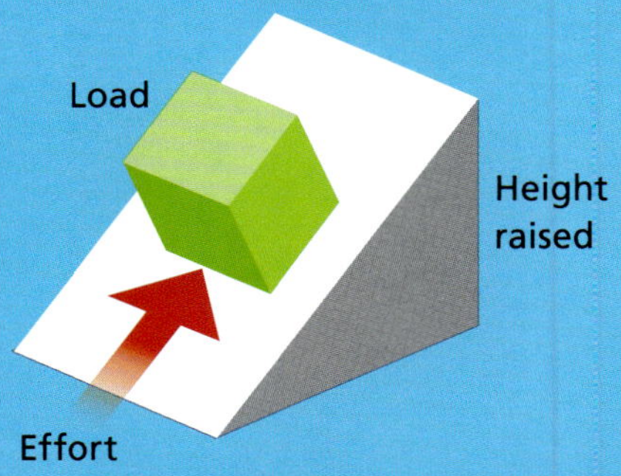

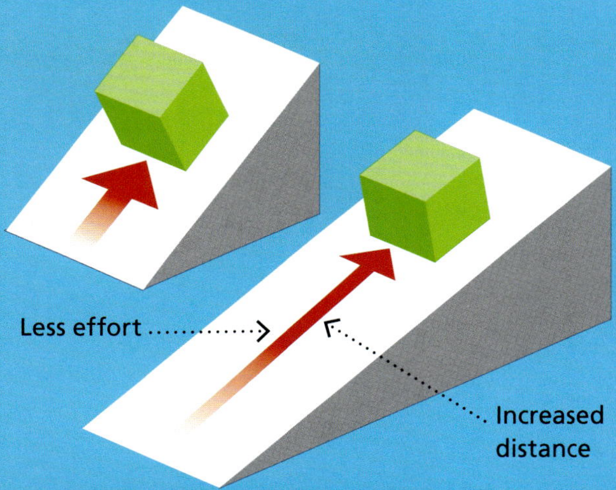

MAKING IT EASIER

The effect of an inclined plane is increased by making the plane longer, so the angle of the incline is less. This reduces the force needed, but increases the distance the object has to be moved.

Ramps are used to ...

SCREWS

A screw transforms a turning movement into a vertical movement.

Screws are used to...

1) Join two objects

2) Lift objects – **a spiral staircase**

3) Fix objects together – **a screw or a nut and bolt**

4) Drill holes – **a drill**

5) Create thrust –

a ship's propeller

6) Close an opening – **a water tap**

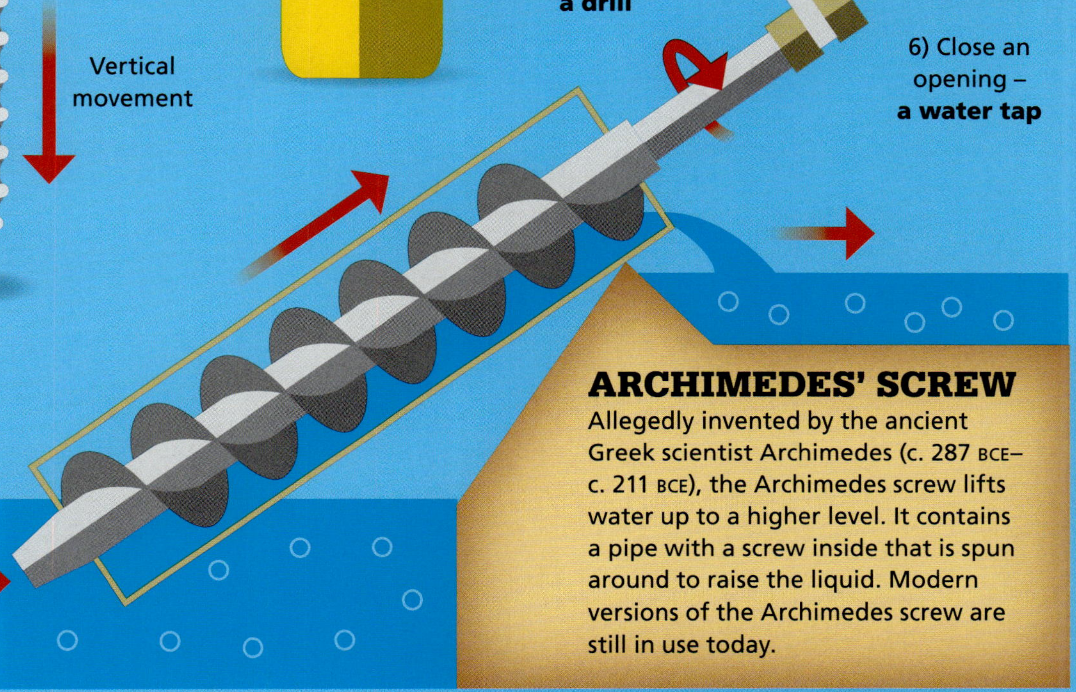

ARCHIMEDES' SCREW

Allegedly invented by the ancient Greek scientist Archimedes (c. 287 BCE–c. 211 BCE), the Archimedes screw lifts water up to a higher level. It contains a pipe with a screw inside that is spun around to raise the liquid. Modern versions of the Archimedes screw are still in use today.

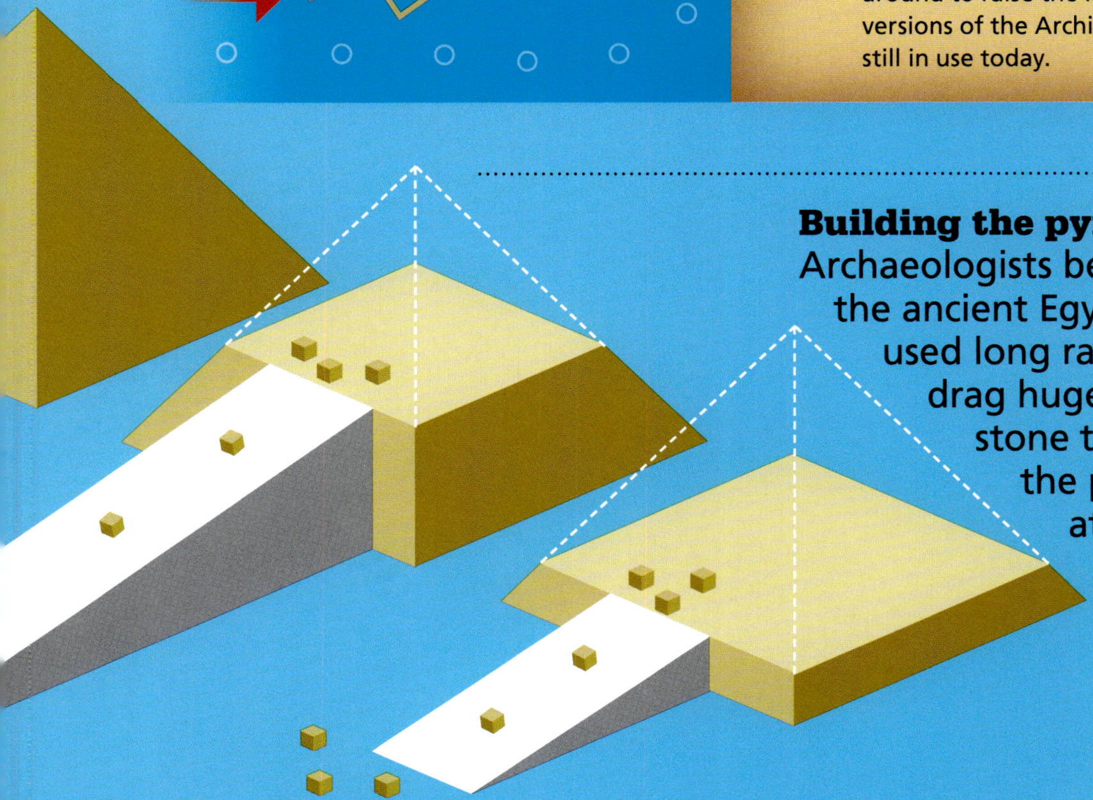

Building the pyramids

Archaeologists believe that the ancient Egyptians used long ramps to drag huge blocks of stone to build the pyramids at Giza.

WHEELS AND PULLEYS

Wheels act as circular levers, moving a force around a central fulcrum (see pages 18–19), called an axle. They also reduce friction by rolling over surfaces to move objects and loads (see pages 8–9). Pulleys use sets of wheels to make lifting and pulling loads easier.

WHEELS AND AXLES

A wheel is a circular disc that rotates around a central axle. Instead of having to overcome friction between the vehicle and the surface it travels over, wheels only have to overcome the friction between the smooth surface of the wheel as it spins around the smooth surface of the axle.

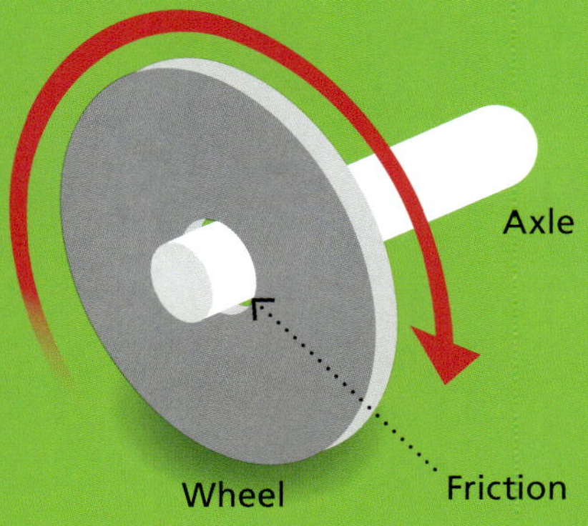

The earliest wheels were used to turn clay and make pots. They first appeared about **10,000 years ago.**

Using wheels

Just like levers, wheels can be used to magnify a force. The rim of a large wheel will turn a greater amount than the rim of a small wheel. Turn a large wheel at the rim and the force is magnified at the axle. If you turn a large wheel at the axle, then the force is decreased at the rim.

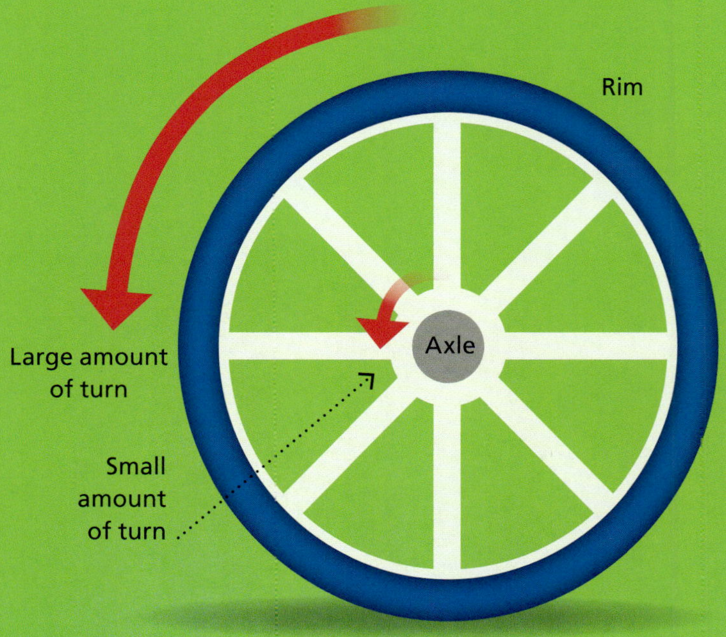

Pulleys

Pulleys are made up of a series of wheels around which a rope is looped.

One wheel
The wheel changes the direction of the force needed to lift an object, but you will need to use a force that is equivalent to the weight of the object.

Two wheels
Adding more wheels reduces the amount of effort needed to lift a load. Using two wheels halves the amount of effort needed, but you have to pull the rope twice the distance.

Four wheels
Using four wheels means that you only have to use a quarter of the effort to lift the load, but the distance you have to pull the rope quadruples.

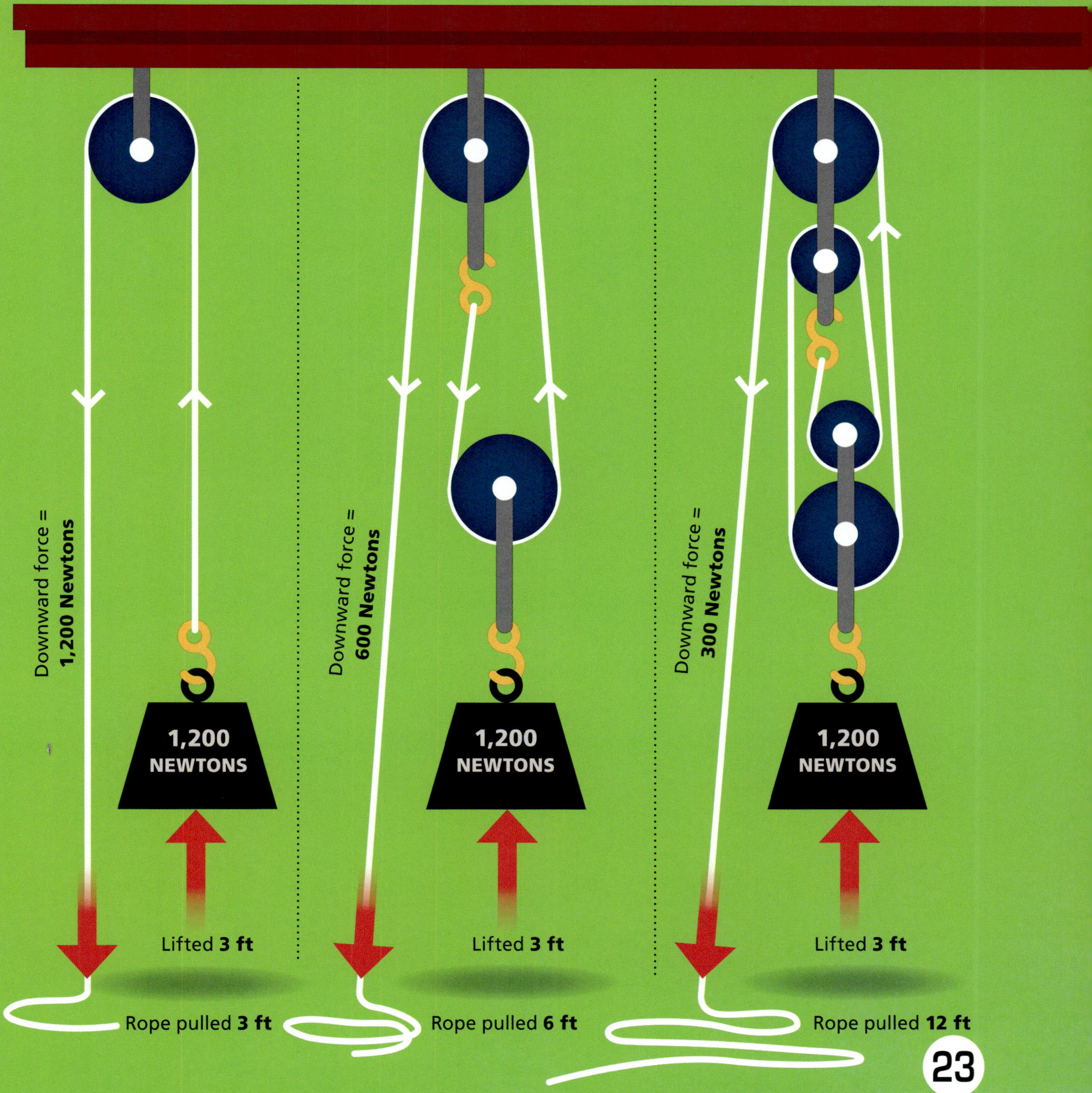

ATOMIC FORCES

Atoms are some of the smallest and most basic pieces of matter in the universe, but they pack a powerful punch. They can be used to help heal people and to generate electricity.

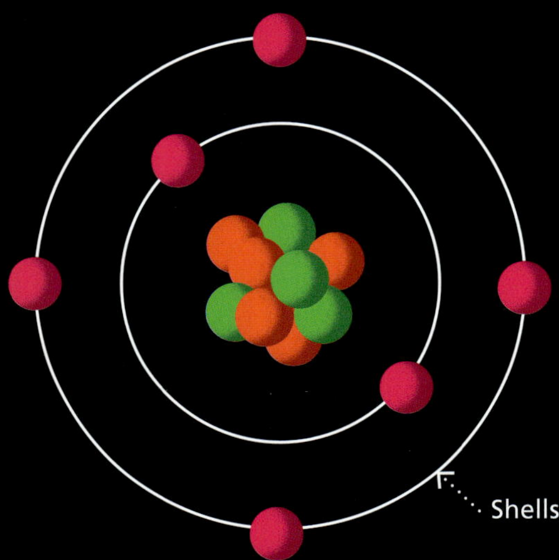

INSIDE ATOMS

At the heart of an atom is a tightly packed group of neutrons and protons. Whizzing around these in shells are tiny electrons.

Electrons have a negative charge.

Protons have a positive charge.

Neutrons have no charge.

1 ton

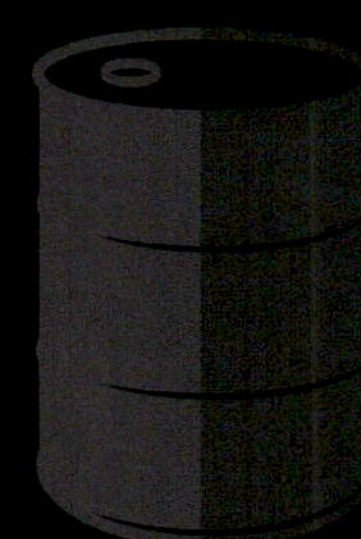

149 gallons

1 pellet

Nuclear fission is used in nuclear reactors to produce electricity. **1 uranium fuel pellet** can produce as much power as **149 gallons of oil** or **1 ton of coal.**

Splitting atoms

Firing a tiny neutron into a large uranium atom will split the uranium atom apart, releasing energy. When the atom splits, it releases more neutrons, which whiz off and split more atoms, releasing more energy and more neutrons, causing a chain reaction. This is called nuclear fission.

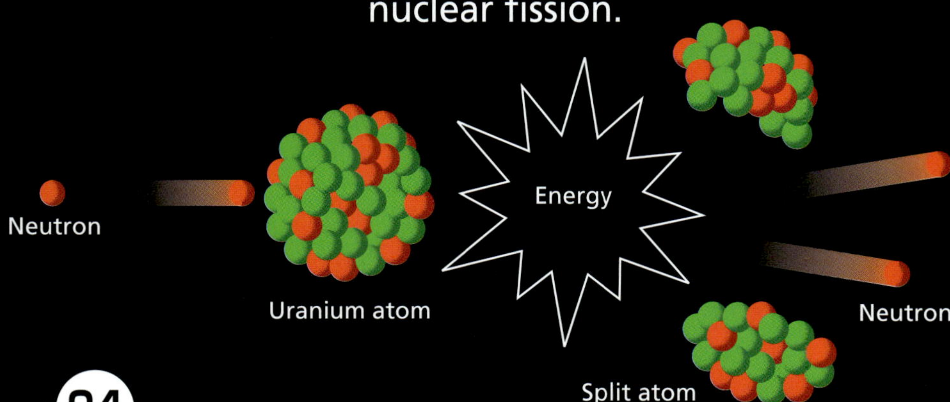

FUSING ATOMS AND SHINING STARS

At the heart of stars, like our sun, huge levels of gravity and high temperatures squeeze atoms together, fusing them to form new atoms. This nuclear fusion also releases energy that we can feel and see as light and heat.

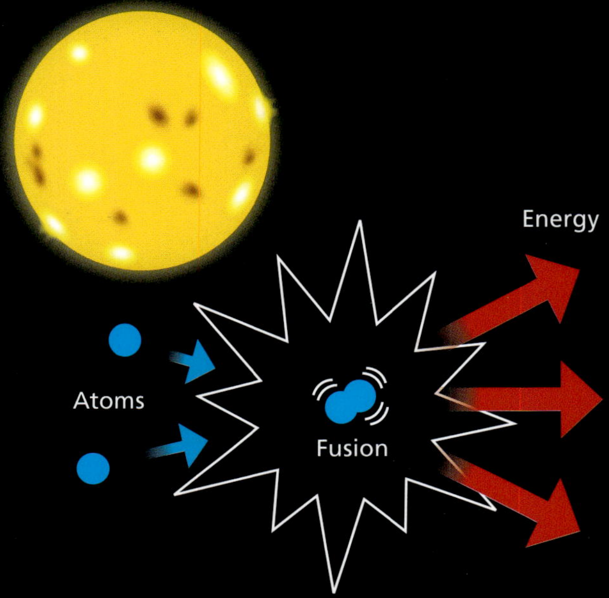

Radioactivity

Some atoms are unstable – they break apart more quickly than stable atoms. When they break apart, these atoms give off radioactivity as small pieces of atoms, such as alpha and beta particles, or as waves of energy called gamma rays.

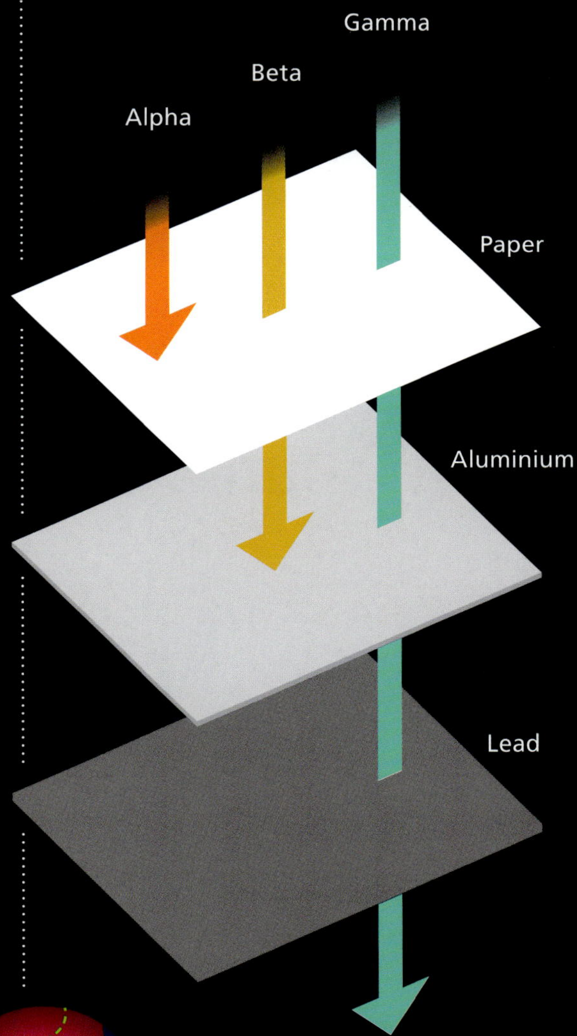

Using radioactivity

Radiation has many uses in modern medicine:

Gamma rays from radioactive materials can be focused onto a growth of cancer cells, called a tumor. The rays kill off the cells.

Gamma rays are used to kill off bacteria and viruses that may be on medical equipment, making them sterile and safe to use.

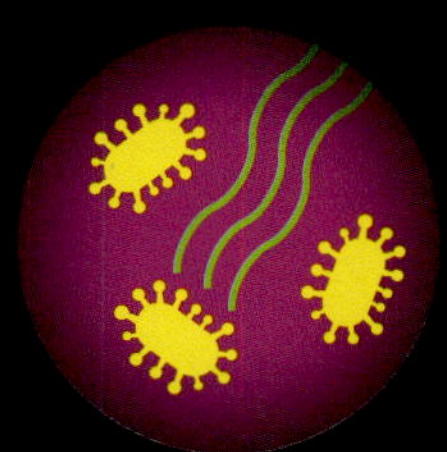

Radioactive materials can be used as tracers, showing how some parts of the body are working.

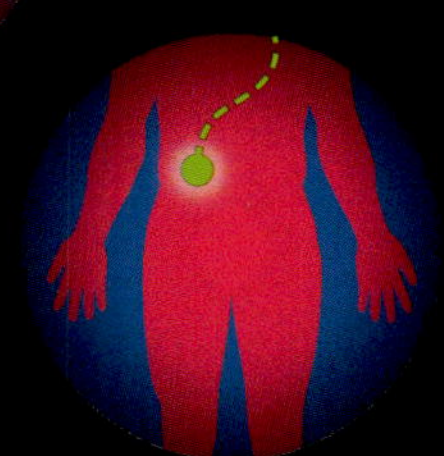

MAGNETS AND MAGNETISM

Magnetism is a natural force that can attract objects or push them away. Magnets can come in all shapes and sizes, from tiny nails to entire planets.

WHAT IS A MAGNET?

A magnet is an object that produces a magnetic field. This field produces a force that can act on other magnetic objects, as well as electrical currents. A magnet has two ends, or poles: a north–or north-seeking–pole, and a south–or south-seeking–pole.

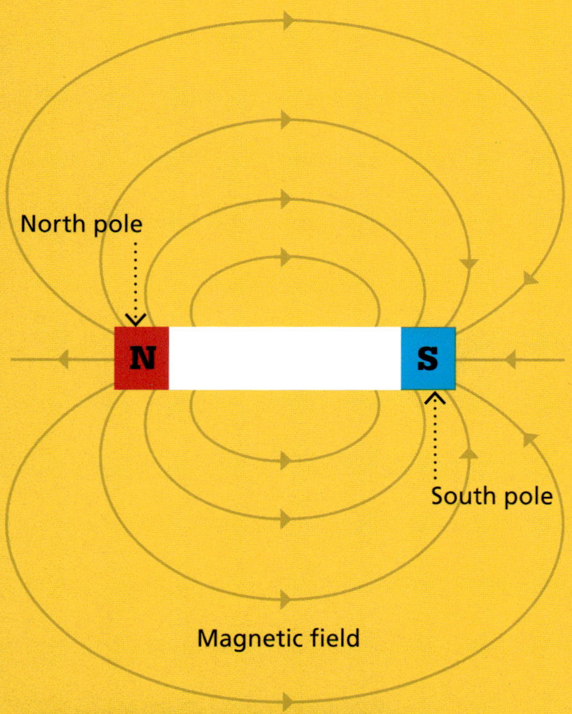

ATTRACT AND REPEL

If the same poles (north and north, or south and south) are brought together, they will push away, or repel, each other. If different poles (north and south) are brought together, they will attract each other.

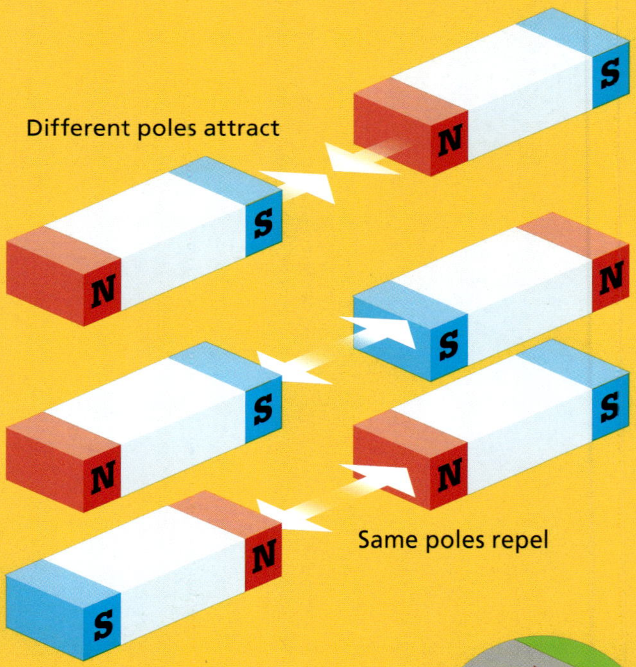

MAKING MAGNETS

Some objects, such as an iron nail, can be made magnetic by stroking a magnet against them. Stroking the nail rearranges the magnetic fields of the iron atoms so they point in the same way. In other objects, the atoms are held too rigidly together and the magnetic fields of their atoms cannot be rearranged.

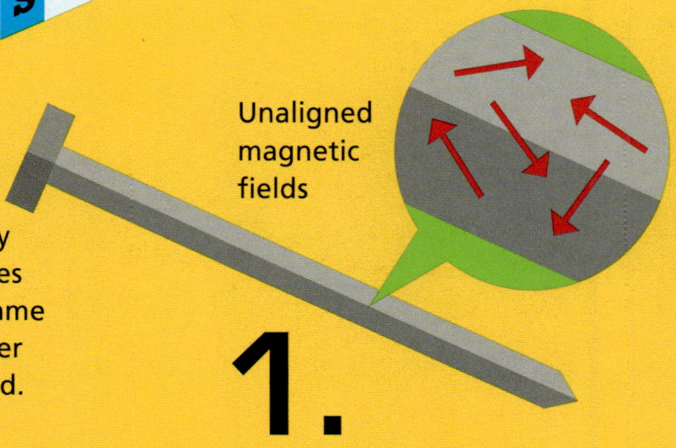

ELECTROMAGNETS

As an electric current flows through a wire, it creates a magnetic field. You can make this magnetic field stronger by wrapping the wire around an iron core, such as a nail.

Planet-sized magnets

Deep inside Earth, high temperature and huge pressures create swirling currents in a superhot soup of liquid metals, such as iron and nickel. As these metals swirl about, they produce a magnetic field, which proves very helpful, even lifesaving, to us.

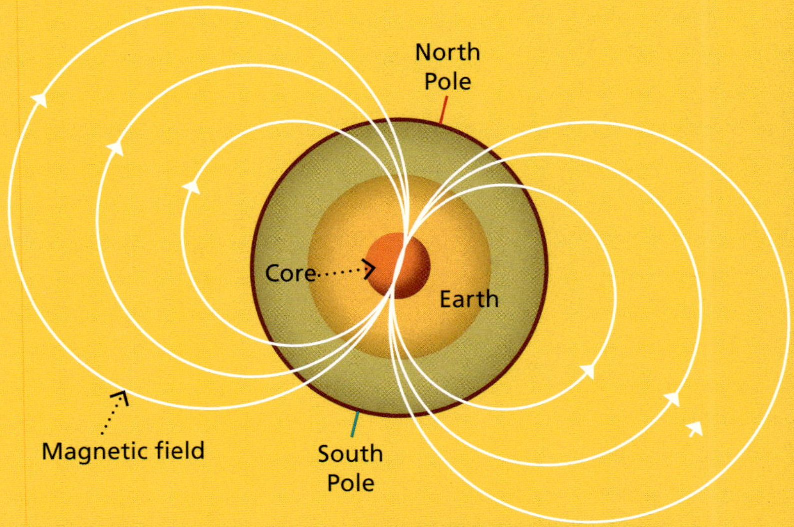

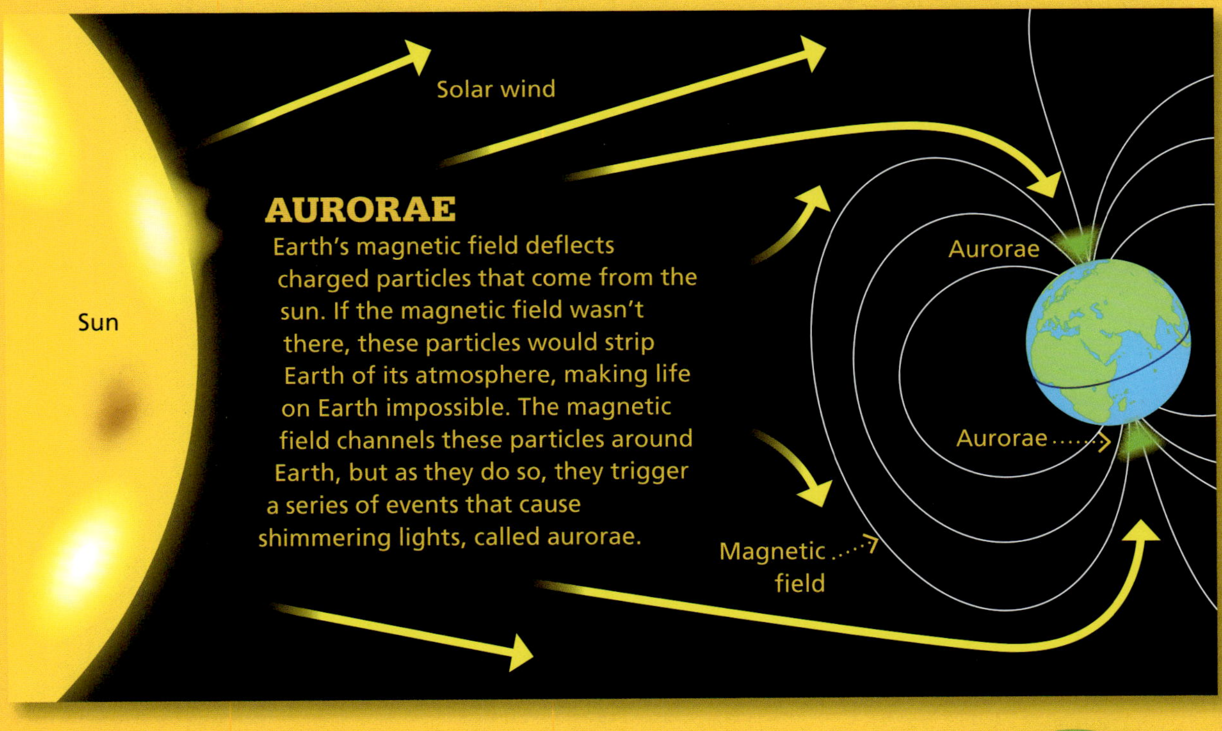

AURORAE

Earth's magnetic field deflects charged particles that come from the sun. If the magnetic field wasn't there, these particles would strip Earth of its atmosphere, making life on Earth impossible. The magnetic field channels these particles around Earth, but as they do so, they trigger a series of events that cause shimmering lights, called aurorae.

2.

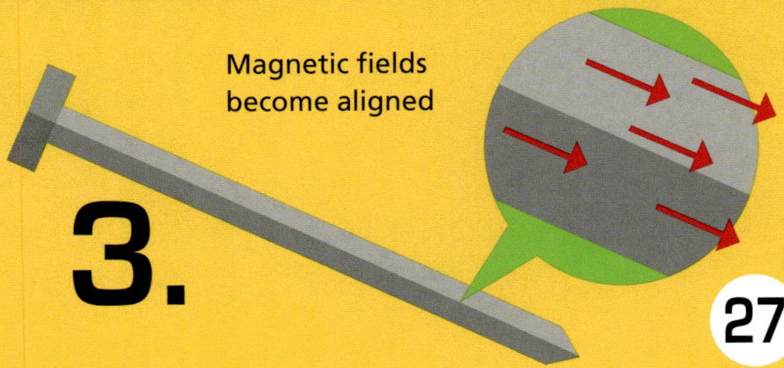

3.

USING MAGNETS

Magnets and magnetism can be used to tell us which way to go and how fast Earth is moving. They can also produce electricity and move things around with incredible force and speed.

Compasses

A compass contains a small magnetized needle that can spin around freely. As it spins around, the needle lines up with Earth's magnetic field, pointing the way to the magnetic north pole.

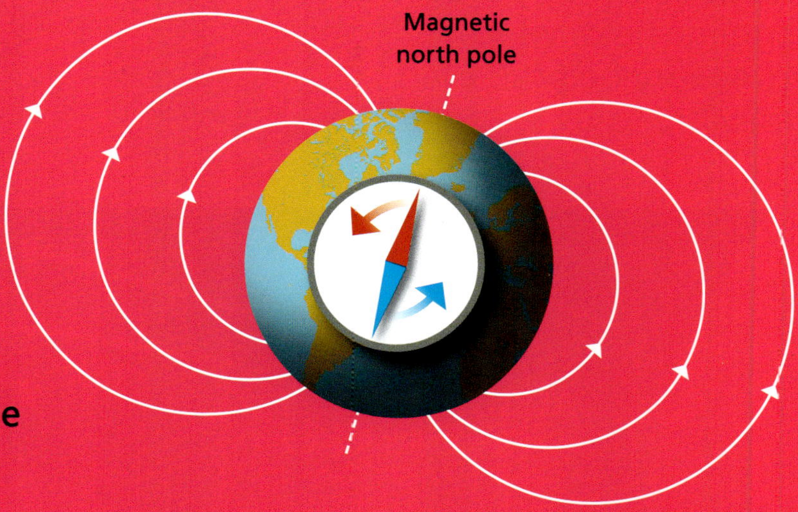

STRIPING ROCKS

As some of Earth's tectonic plates pull apart, molten rock wells up from under the surface. As the rock cools, the particles inside it line up with Earth's magnetic field. Every 250,000 years or so, Earth's magnetic field reverses, so the north and south magnetic poles swap positions. Any new liquid rock that erupts then takes on the opposite magnetic pattern to the rock next to it, producing magnetic "stripes" in the rocks.

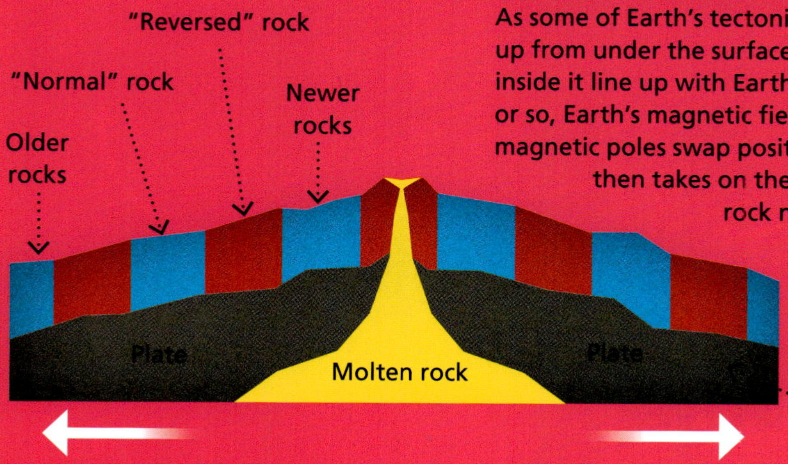

Scientists can use these "stripes" to calculate the age of the rock and how quickly the tectonic plates moved.

We are overdue for a reversal of Earth's magnetic field, as the last one happened some **780,000 years ago.**

Making electricity

By spinning a metal coil in a magnetic field, you can produce an electric current. This principle is used inside electrical generators to turn the movement of steam, water, and even wind to produce the power we need to run our homes and businesses.

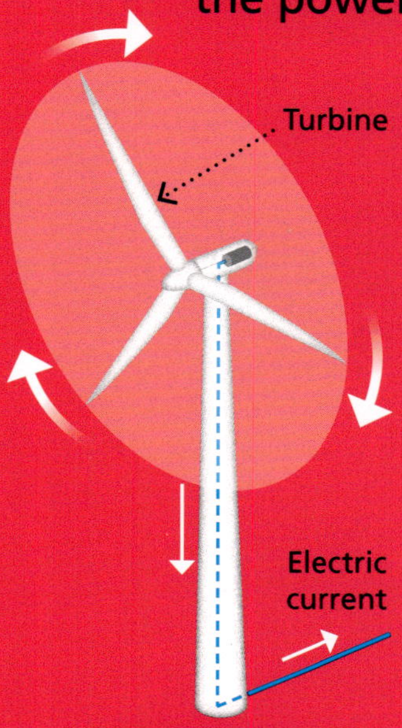

Wind turbine

WIND POWER

A wind turbine harnesses the movement of air to spin its huge blades. These blades are attached to large coils that spin around in a magnetic field inside a generator to produce an electric current.

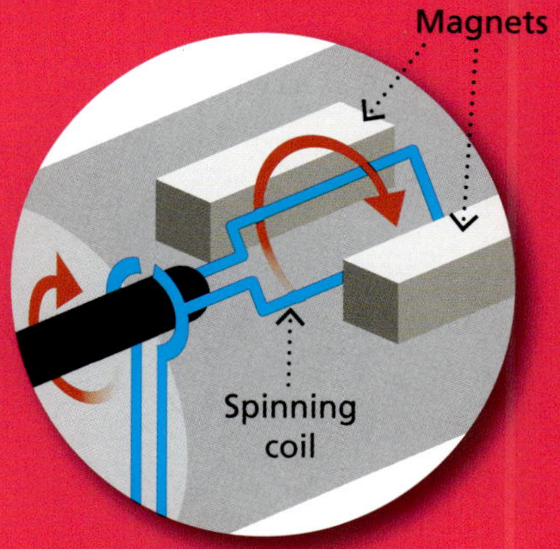

Electric generator

WATER POWER

Water can be used to make electricity in a number of ways. Hydroelectric dams use flowing water to spin turbines connected to generators (see page 6), while wave and tidal generators use the moving seawater.

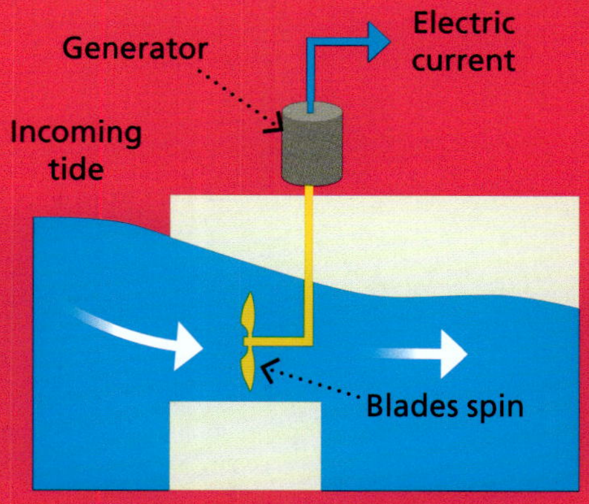

Tidal power

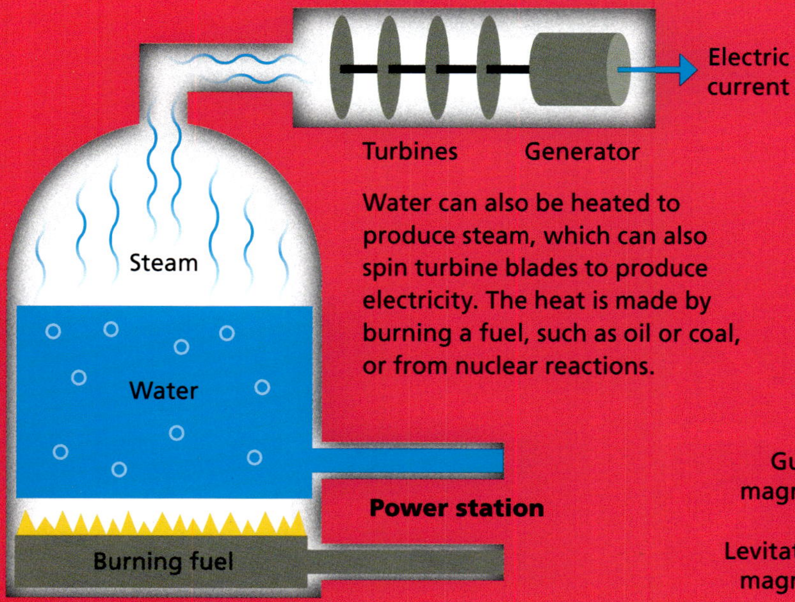

Power station

Water can also be heated to produce steam, which can also spin turbine blades to produce electricity. The heat is made by burning a fuel, such as oil or coal, or from nuclear reactions.

MAGLEV

Maglev trains use the repelling force of magnets to make the trains float above the track. In doing so, they remove any friction between the train and the track, allowing the train to zoom along at speeds of nearly 375 miles (603 km) per hour.

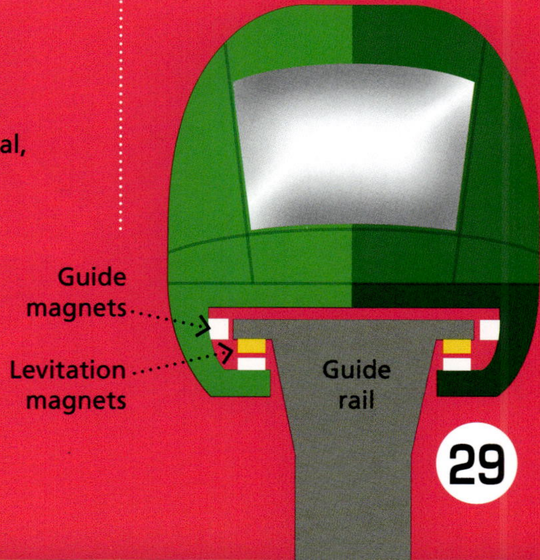

GLOSSARY

acceleration
When something gets faster and faster.

air resistance
A force that acts in the opposite direction to the one an object is moving in. It is produced by the surface of the object rubbing against air molecules.

angle of attack
The angle at which a wing is set.

atmospheric pressure
Pressure produced by air pushing on an object.

aurorae
Bands of colored lights that occur high in the atmosphere close to the polar regions. They are caused by charged particles from the sun interacting with molecules in the air.

axle
A rod that runs through the middle of a wheel and around which the wheel rotates.

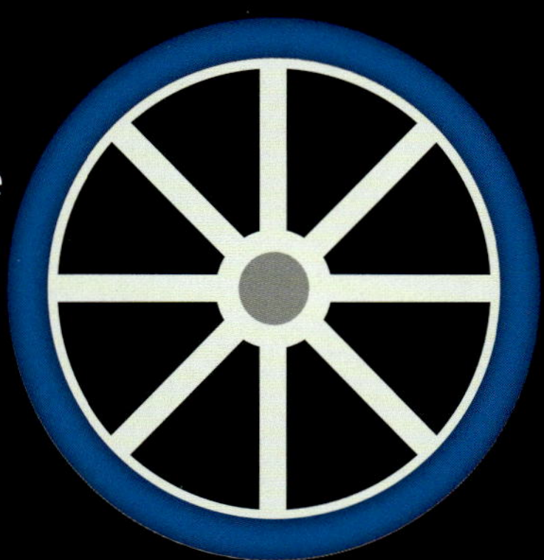

deceleration
When something gets slower and slower. Scientists sometimes call it negative acceleration.

downforce
A force produced by a flow of air which pushes a vehicle down into the ground. Race cars use downforce to improve their grip on the road.

electromagnet
A magnet that produces a magnetic field by passing an electric current through a wire coil that has been wrapped around a metal core.

friction
A force produced by two objects rubbing against each other. This force makes any movement harder.

fulcrum
A pivot around which a lever rotates.

generator
A machine that produces electricity, usually by spinning a wire coil in a magnetic field.

gravity
A force that attracts one object with mass to another object with mass. The more mass an object has, the greater its gravitational force.

hydraulics
The study of how liquids and gases behave. Hydraulic machines use liquids to transmit forces to carry out work.

inclined plane

A type of simple machine that has a slope which can be used to raise or lower objects.

lever

A type of simple machine that uses a rod which rotates around a fulcrum to lift a load.

lift

The force used to raise a plane into the air. It is produced by the movement of air over the wings.

lubricant

A substance that sits between two surfaces and reduces the amount of friction between them as they rub together.

magnetic pole

One of two ends of a magnet.

mass

The amount of material an object or substance is made from.

orbit

The path of one object around another object.

pressure

The force produced when one object pushes on another.

pulley

A type of simple machine that uses wheels and ropes to make lifting or pulling objects easier.

screw

A type of simple machine that has an inclined plane wrapped around a central core.

streamlined

A shape that is designed to move through air or water easily.

turbine

A wheel that is made up of individual blades.

Websites

MORE INFO:

www.scienceforkidsclub.com/push-and-pull.html
This web page is packed full of amazing facts about forces, as well as hands-on experiments and links to web pages on other science topics.

www.science-sparks.com/2014/01/29/ideas-for-learning-about-forces/
This website is packed with science facts and projects.

MORE GRAPHICS:

elearninginfographics.com/category/k12-infographics/elementary-school-infographics/
This web page has tons of school-related infographics.

www.kidsdiscover.com/infographics
This website contains a whole host of infographic material on many different subjects.

Publisher's note to educators and parents: Our editors have carefully reviewed these websites to ensure that they are suitable for students. Many websites change frequently, however, and we cannot guarantee that a site's future contents will continue to meet our high standards of quality and educational value. Be advised that students should be closely supervised whenever they access the Internet.

INDEX

acceleration 12–13
air resistance 10, 11
Archimedes screw 21
atoms 24, 25
aurorae 27

brakes 9

catamarans 11
compasses 28

Earth 4, 5, 6, 7
Earth's magnetic field 27, 28
electromagnets 27

friction 8–9

generators 6, 29
gravity 4–5, 6, 7, 11, 12, 13

hydraulics 16
hydroelectric power station 6, 29
hydrofoil 11

Jupiter 4, 5

levers 18, 19
lift 17
lubrication 8

maglev trains 29
magnets 26–27, 28, 29
Mars 5
mass 4
Mercury 5
moon 11

Neptune 6
New Horizons 7
Newton, Isaac 4
nuclear fission 24
nuclear fusion 25

orbit 4, 5

parachutes 11
Pluto 7
pressure 14–15, 16, 17
pulleys 23

radioactivity 25
ramps 20, 21
rockets 6, 13

Saturn 5
screws 19
skating 9
streamlining 10
sun 5, 7, 25

thumbtacks 17
tractor tires 17
trimarans 11
turbine 6

Uranus 5

Venus 5

water mill 6
weather 16
wedges 18, 19
weight 4
wheels 9, 22, 23
wings 17
wing turbine 29